The next thing I knew, Ms. Rappitz was introducing me. Rex had returned to his seat next to me, his face flushed with success. "Go get 'em," he said as I walked toward the stage. I felt as if I couldn't breathe at all, and I could feel my whole body trembling. I didn't even know if I could stand up! I felt a terrible panic come over me. But once I got up on the stage and saw Ms. Thomason's smiling face nodding encouragement to me from behind the piano, some confidence returned. I took a deep breath from way down in my chest, and nodded at her to start the accompaniment.

ALLIE'S BIG BREAK

by Carrie Austen

SPLASH™

B

A BERKLEY / SPLASH BOOK

THE PARTY LINE #5: ALLIE'S BIG BREAK is an original publication
of the Berkley Publishing Group. This work has never appeared before
in book form.

A Berkley Book/published by arrangement with
General Licensing Company, Inc.

PRINTING HISTORY
Berkley edition/September 1990

A GLC BOOK

ISBN: 0-425-12266-2
RL: 5.3

A BERKLEY BOOK® TM 757,375
Berkley Books are published by
The Berkley Publishing Group,
200 Madison Avenue, New York, New York 10016.
The name "Berkley" and the "B" logo are trademarks belonging to
Berkley Publishing Corporation.

PRINTED IN THE UNITED STATES OF AMERICA

10 9 8 7 6 5 4 3 2 1

ALLIE'S BIG BREAK

One

"Earth to Allie! Earth to Allie!" Julie Berger was calling to me from the front seat of her mom's car. "Honestly, Allie, you've been staring out that window for five minutes!"

"I have?"

Rosie Torres was sitting next to me in the back seat. She leaned over me to look out my window. "Well, County Road looks the same as usual. There's the McDonald's, and, yup, the good old Seven-Eleven—but wait! Who's that in the car next to us? Yes! It's Michael J. Fox, waving to Allie! You've got to pull over, Mrs. Berger!"

Mrs. Berger just smiled and kept driving. Julie and Rosie laughed, and I stuck out my tongue at them. I swear, they must lie awake at night thinking up new ways to tease me. I don't mind, though—we're all really great friends.

"Actually, I was going over the details for the

party in my mind, so I don't forget anything," I said with mock indignation.

Julie laughed. "Allison Gray, you're so organized you'd never forget anything!"

"The party will be great, Allie. Don't worry!" said Rosie. "We'll have a blast. What eight-year-old doesn't love to roller-skate?"

Julie laughed. "What thirteen-year-old doesn't love to roller-skate?" All four of us have taken skating lessons and we're pretty good, especially Julie and Rosie.

Mrs. Berger pulled into the parking lot of the Moondance Café and my very best friend in the world, Becky Bartlett, came running down the brick path. Becky's parents own the Moondance and her family lives above the restaurant. "Hi, you guys," she said as she climbed into the back of Mrs. Berger's car. "I'm so psyched for this party!"

It was Sunday afternoon and the four of us were on our way to the Roxy Roller Rink, right next door to the Pine Tree Mall. We were giving a birthday party for Patti Jackson, who was turning eight years old. A couple of days earlier I had gotten a frantic call from Patti's mom. She had been intending to throw a small party at the Jacksons' house, but Patti's little sister had come down with the chickenpox! Luckily, Patti is a friend of my sister Caroline, who is also eight, and Caroline told her about our party business, The Party Line.

The whole idea for The Party Line got started a few months ago, when the clown my parents had hired for my little brother Mouse's birthday party called in sick at the last minute. When Rosie, Julie, Becky, and I got back from the mall that day, we walked into a total zoo! Little kids were running all over the place, crying and screaming, and my mom looked like she was in a state of shock. Without really thinking about it, the four of us pitched in to help, and everyone ended up having a fabulous time.

A few days after Mouse's party I got a phone call from the mother of one of the kids who had been at the party. She said her son just wouldn't stop talking about what a wonderful time he'd had, and then she said she wanted to hire me and my friends to give a birthday party for her daughter. Hire! As in *money*. As in *get paid*. I could hardly believe it. I said I'd have to check with my friends, and of course the first person I called was Becky. She immediately loved the idea. In fact, then and there she thought up the idea that the four of us should start an actual business giving parties.

It was amazing how quickly our business took off. Not that we didn't make mistakes—especially at first! For example, I'm the vice president and I'm in charge of keeping track of the details for each party. Well, for our very first party I forgot to add our profit into the budget, and we nearly ended up doing the party for free. Everything worked out fine in the end, but it really does bug me to make mistakes. My friends say I'm a perfectionist and my dad is always telling me to lighten up, but I just hate it when I feel like I didn't do my best.

We usually hold Party Line meetings every Sunday in Becky's attic. (Of course, that Sunday we were already busy with the skating, so we'd had a mobile meeting the day before while we shopped for last-minute supplies.) Becky's attic is a really cool place full of old trunks and boxes. We spent a lot of time cleaning it up and decorating it with posters and pillows and stuff. It's wonderful to have our own special headquarters, someplace that really belongs to us.

Becky is president, since The Party Line was her idea. She's also just a natural-born leader. She's very creative and comes up with the greatest ideas for parties. To tell the truth, Becky is a bit klutzy, though. (Her brother David calls her a walking disaster area.) Her parents never used to let her near the china or knives in the Moondance, but since they've seen how successful she's been with The Party Line, they're starting to let her do a little more than just restock the restaurant's salad bar. Actually, I've always thought that Becky is just so full of great ideas that sometimes she gets carried away and doesn't concentrate on what she's doing. Not all of her great ideas work, but I bet that was true of every great creative thinker in history. I really do admire how spontaneous she is, and sometimes I wish I could be a little less serious and a little more like her.

Rosie is our treasurer, because she's so great in math. She's also an artist; she designs all our flyers and comes up with most of the ideas for party decorations. Maybe because she's so artistic, she's always experimenting with clothes and makeup and she always looks terrific. She's constantly trying out new ideas on the three of us, too—we can't pass the makeup counter at Winter's without at least one of us leaving with an entirely different look.

Julie is our official secretary and takes notes at all our meetings. What Julie really excels at, though, is anything to do with sports. She's a fabulous baseball player and wants to play in the major leagues someday. Ask Julie a question about a ballplayer's statistics and she'll know the answer. Some of the guys at Canfield Middle School, which is where we all go, get bent out of shape at how good Julie is. If you ask me, boys like that are dumb. Lately, though, some of them have actually started to ask her to play on their teams, which is great. Julie's really enthusiastic, too, which is a big help at our parties. It's impossible for kids to be around her and not have a good time.

Julie was going to lead most of the games we had planned for Patti's party at the roller rink. We'd gotten some great party favors, too, like keychains with small day-glo roller skates attached to them. Becky and I had even found some great cookie cutters in the shape of roller skates, and after we made a couple of batches of sugar cookies we used white frosting on the boot part and chocolate glaze for the wheels and laces. That's what I mean about Becky being creative—the rollerskate cookies were all her idea.

As we got closer to the Roxy, I pulled a list out of my notebook. "I think we should go over the checklist for the party before we get there," I said.

Rosie rolled her eyes. Sometimes it drives her nuts when I check things so many times to make sure they're right.

"We did it over the phone last night," Rosie reminded me. "Nothing's changed."

"Double-checking is a good idea," Becky said, defending me.

But Julie wasn't much interested in double-checking, either, and she turned up the radio so that we could hear it better in the back seat.

"Hey, Allie, it's that great new Vermilion song!"

I immediately forgot all about my checklist and asked Julie to turn up the volume even more. As far as I'm concerned, Vermilion is the greatest singer who ever lived. All my friends like Vermilion, but I adore her. See, what I really love to do is sing. My friends are always telling me that I have a great voice, but my problem is that when I think about singing in front of people I just freeze up. I have this problem with shyness, and sometimes if I'm really nervous or self-conscious I even stutter a little, which is completely mortifying. But I'm trying to overcome it, because I know that when Vermilion was younger she was really shy, too, and she even stuttered!

Sometimes when I'm alone in the room I share with my sister, I sing the lyrics to Vermilion's songs and practice the dance steps I see her do in her videos. The only person who's ever seen me do that is Becky, and she thinks I look and sound really good. The problem is, I'd never have the nerve to do it in front of anyone but Becky.

My three friends started singing along with Vermilion on the radio and I joined in. Mrs. Berger even started to hum the melody, she had heard it so many times. I tried to sing harmony on a few notes, the way we were learning to do in music class, and it sounded great. I read in *Saucy* magazine that Vermilion sings harmony with herself on records. It's called overdubbing. The article said that first she records the melody, then as she listens to the melody through headphones she sings a harmony part over it.

"Great harmony!" said Becky, smiling at my effort. "Just like Vermilion!"

"I think it's wicked cool that you got to meet Vermilion," said Rosie dreamily.

Amazing as it seems, I actually *had* met Vermilion! She was doing a concert at Taylor College and she came into the Moondance with her dad for dinner. Becky's mom told Vermilion about me, and Vermilion invited me and Becky backstage after the concert! It was like a dream come true. Even as I was standing there talking to Vermilion, I was thinking that it wasn't really happening, that I was dreaming and soon I'd wake up and find out I'd been talking to my pillow. I actually had to pinch my own arm during the conversation, just to prove to myself that it was real! And she was so nice, just like a regular person. The word got around school fast that I had met Vermilion, and everyone had a million questions: was she a snob, how was she dressed, things like that. To this day I can recall every moment of that evening. Sometimes I play it over in my mind, like some wonderful movie but even better, because it actually happened.

I shut my eyes, remembering how wonderful it had been, and sang along with Vermilion on the radio. I got so much into the music that I didn't notice when my three friends and Mrs. Berger stopped singing. When Vermilion and I finished singing, Julie, Rosie, and Becky broke into applause. Julie even whistled through her teeth the way they do at big rock concerts.

"No lie, that was great, Allie!" cried Rosie.

I shrugged away the compliment.

"You really do have a terrific voice, Allie," said Mrs. Berger, looking at me in the rearview mirror.

"You sing better than Marsha Clark and she gets all the solos in chorus," said Julie.

"I don't! She's got a great voice!" I protested.

Julie shook her head at me. "The problem with you, Allie, is that you don't appreciate how totally amazing you are."

"Yeah, right" I snorted.

"It's true!" said Julie. "You have mega-talent."

"Oh, that reminds me," said Becky as she fished a piece of paper out of her coat pocket. "Look at this flyer. I found this posted on the bulletin board at the mall."

I leaned over to read the flyer.

WCAN-TV Talent Search, said the headline.

Rosie grabbed the flyer from Becky and read it out loud. " 'WCAN-TV is sponsoring a talent search for young people, ages twelve to sixteen. If you have a special talent, we want you to share it with us! The grand prize winner will appear on WCAN-TV.' Then the flyer tells how to register and who to call for more details."

My friends got really excited. "This is it, Allie!" cried Becky. "This could be your big break!"

"You guys—" I started to say.

"Wow, a career launched in the back of my mom's car," Julie marveled.

"Get out of here!" I said with a laugh.

Rosie pointed one perfect pink fingernail at me. "I'm totally serious, Allie. You could end up on TV!"

I made a face. "Forget it, you guys. I could never do it in a million years!"

"Let's call and find out what she needs to do to enter," suggested Rosie.

Becky grinned. "I already did. What you have to do is to have a teacher from school recommend you. The teacher writes a letter about you and then you send the letter in with the entry blank."

"Well, Allie, what do you say?" asked Julie.

I looked at my friends, who were staring at me. "I say you guys are crazy!" I laughed.

Mrs. Berger pulled into the parking lot at the Roxy, and we all thanked her for the ride and piled out of the car. I was the last one out and Mrs. Berger stopped me for a moment, leaning her head out the car window.

"You know, Allie, I agree with them. You sing so well it would be a shame not to try." Then she smiled at me and drove off.

I stared after Mrs. Berger's car until I was startled by Rosie screaming, "Hey, race you to the door!" Julie and Becky ran after Rosie but I lagged behind, lost in thought. When I had met Vermilion she told me to follow my dream. Well, it seemed to me it was one thing to have big dreams and quite another to try to make them come true.

Still, hadn't being a professional singer once been only a dream to Vermilion? She hadn't stopped herself from trying, that was for sure. And I remembered that my mom had told me once that the only failure is not to try at all. What if I did actually try ... and what if I won? I imagined what it could be like—me, actually singing on TV. My parents would be there, and all my brothers and sisters. All the kids in school would be there, too, even a certain boy named Dylan Matthews.

Dylan would come up to me after the show. He'd look at me the way I looked at Vermilion when I went backstage after her concert. I'd look really gorgeous in some to-die-for outfit, and Dylan would hold out a notebook and a pen, hoping for my autograph.

I was in such a daze from my daydream that I didn't notice this really cute guy wearing a Canfield High jacket walking toward me across the parking lot. He was in the middle of a conversation with two of his friends. *Boom!* We collided head-on. I dropped my Party Line notebook and papers flew everywhere.

The cute guy laughed and helped me pick up my stuff. I turned about a million shades of red, and I felt like I had swallowed pillow stuffing.

"S-sorry. I d-didn't see you," I gulped out.

He smiled at me. "No harm done."

I had *stuttered*. Right then my dream burst like a big piece of bubble gum, and I wanted to crawl into a hole and die. Who did I think I was, anyway? I was just plain Allie Gray, and I could never, ever sing in the contest or be on TV. I must have been crazy even to think about entering that contest!

Two

We had arrived at the Roxy a half-hour before we expected the kids, so we could set everything up. The manager of the Roxy had given us a special section of the roller rink to use when the kids weren't skating. There we put up this great multi-colored Happy Birthday Patti banner that Rosie had designed. We blew up balloons and hung streamers until everything looked perfect.

When the birthday girl arrived she was proudly carrying a present from her parents, who had given it to her early in honor of her skating party: a pair of gleaming white roller skates with day-glo pink laces. The top of the skates had a band of pink-and-white polka-dot ribbon. Only one or two of the other little girls had their own skates and they all gathered around to look at Patti's. My sister Caroline came in with her best friend, Mindy. They wore matching sweaters and since they look a lot alike anyway, they almost could have been mistaken for twins. Caroline hadn't wanted to come to the rink early with me because she thought it was kind of dweeby to have her older sister at a party, but she was really excited about the roller skating and she flashed me a quick smile when she thought no one else was looking.

"Come on, kids, time to get in line for skates," called Julie. Most of the kids would be renting their skates, which came in either scuffed grayish white or dull black. They looked covetously back at Patti's brilliantly white pair and sighed as we helped them pick out the right size. Samantha Chapin, a little girl with a long black ponytail, hadn't put on her own pair of rented black skates and was trying to get Patti to let her wear Patti's new ones. "I'll give them right back," she wheedled.

Becky walked over to her. "I know Patti's skates are beautiful, but they belong to Patti. It *is* her birthday," Becky explained patiently.

Samantha stood with her small fists clenched and stared at Becky. "So what?"

"So she gets to wear her skates. Come on, I'll help you lace yours up," Becky offered.

Samantha gave an exaggerated sigh and sat down on a bench so that Becky could help her lace up her skates.

I caught Becky's eye and shook my head. We

knew we couldn't let the party turn into a sulk fest. Becky, Julie, Rosie, and I all had on differently colored T-shirts with our jeans. Once we got the kids laced into their skates, I picked up a pile of hair ribbons in colors that matched our T-shirts.

"Okay, everyone," I called out. "I'm going to pass out hair ribbons to each of you." We had planned that each of us would be in charge of the five little skaters whose hair ribbons matched her T-shirt.

The kids all grabbed at the ribbons, screeching and giggling. "Okay, listen up," called Becky over the excited voices of the children. "Does everyone have their hair ribbon?"

"Yeah!" they all shouted.

A big grin spread over Becky's face. "Great! Now, everyone go stand in front of the team captain whose T-shirt matches your hair ribbon!"

The kids thought this was great fun and they all scrambled around on their skates to stand near the right person. I was captain of the green team, and everything was going fine until Samantha Chapin, who had a green ribbon, started whining.

"Green? I hate green. Green makes me want to barf!" She stuck her lower lip out in a pout and stared at me. Suddenly every girl on the green team hated the color green. "I wanna be blue!" yelled Jennifer Levine. By that time every kid on the green team was screaming about how yucky the color green was. I had to think fast.

"It's too bad you don't like green," I said over their voices, "because we decided that the green team would lead the skating color parade, sort of like in the Olympics. But if you really don't want to be green . . ." I let my voice trail off. The girls looked at one another, and suddenly green was the coolest color to be.

I led the green team out onto the floor. Becky, Rosie, and Julie followed me with their teams. Each team held hands as we skated across the roller rink. The girls looked so cute in their bright tights and sweaters, hair ribbons flying.

Julie led them in formations—"Just like the Ice Capades," she told them, "only on roller skates." Then the girls made a big circle and watched as Julie went into the center of the floor to show them some fancy, difficult skating moves. Finally, Julie took the birthday girl into the center of the circle with her. Julie held Patti's hands and skated around with her, helping her to do all sorts of terrific moves. Patti's cheeks were bright pink and her eyes glistened with happiness and excitement. When the song ended all Patti's friends clapped for her and Julie taught her how to do a deep bow on skates.

After all that skating the kids were really hungry. We went back to our section of the rink and broke out the refreshments. The kids started munching, and Patti began opening her presents between bites. The roller-skate cookies were a huge hit and disappeared as quickly as we put them out.

When Patti had opened all her presents, Becky brought in the birthday cake. We had ordered it from the Moondance's baker, Matthew, who not only makes fantastic cakes but gives us a discount as well! With colored frosting Matthew had created a picture of Patti; it looked just like her, with long blond hair and big blue eyes. But best of all was that on her feet Matthew had put two white roller skates with pink-and-white polka-dot tops. All the girls oohed and ahhed over the cake. Patti cut the first piece of cake herself, with a little help from Becky, and of course we saved the roller-skate part of the cake for the birthday girl to eat.

I looked at the clock, realized we only had time for one last skate, and nudged Julie. She jumped up from the bench. "Okay, kids, it's time for the final birthday skating parade! Everyone form a line behind me, birthday girl first!"

The little girls wobbled and scrambled into a line, with me and Rosie in the middle and Becky bringing up the rear. As luck would have it, the D.J. put on a Vermilion song, "It Takes Rain to Make a Rainbow." As our long parade began to snake around the roller rink, I started singing.

Some people say don't go too fast
It's better to go slow.
But dreamers dream
And darers dare
To follow their own rainbow!

All the little girls joined in on the chorus, singing at the top of their lungs.

It takes rain, rain, rain . . . to make a rainbow!

We continued on like that, me singing all the verses and the kids coming in each time on the chorus, as we paraded around and around the roller rink. The kids looked so happy and I felt just terrific. Even Samantha had a big smile on her face and was singing (sort of screaming) the chorus.

By the time we finished the song, parents were arriving to pick up their kids. Feeling flushed and happy, I started helping the girls get out of their skates. I hummed "It Takes Rain to Make a Rainbow" under my breath. Just as I was helping the last little girl out of her skates, Patti ran up to me and gave me a big hug. "Thanks for the best birthday ever!" she said, just before she ran out the door.

Becky had a huge grin on her face. "Well, I'd say we really outdid ourselves this time."

Julie giggled as she began stuffing torn-up

wrapping paper into the garbage can. "How about that kid, Samantha? What a brat!"

"Don't laugh," said Rosie. "We're liable to get hired to do her party next. Hey, did you see the look on her face when she was watching Allie sing? Rapture, sheer rapture. I bet she thought she was listening to Vermilion herself!"

"Oh, sure," I snorted, but secretly I felt really good that I had won Samantha over. Like I said, I hate it when I don't do my best.

Just as we were finishing dinner that night, I was in the middle of telling my family how great the party had been when the phone rang. My older sister, Suzanne, jumped up to answer it. She's fourteen and assumes that every phone call is for her. She came back into the kitchen looking totally disgusted.

"It's for Allie."

I smiled sweetly at Suzanne and headed for the phone in the front hall. "And don't stay on long," Suzanne yelled after me. "I'm expecting a call." That probably meant she was waiting for her boyfriend, Tommy Piper, to phone.

"Hello?" I said, picking up the receiver.

"Hello, Allie? This is Mrs. Jackson. I want to thank you and your friends for doing such a wonderful job on Patti's party today. She just can't stop talking about it."

"Thanks, Mrs. Jackson. We really had fun, too."

"You know, Allie, Mr. Jackson and I have decided we want to give you girls a bonus, in addition to the balance we owe you."

I wanted to scream "Great!" into the phone, but instead I said, trying to keep the excitement out of my voice, "Gee, that's really not necessary."

I could practically hear her smiling into the phone. "You're right, it isn't necessary, but it's something we'd really like to do. Is it all right if I stop over in, say, an hour with the money?"

"Well, sure, that would be fine, but really—"

"No more protests, Allie. It's my pleasure. See you soon."

I felt so good, I called up Becky right away to tell her about the bonus. I knew Becky would use the phone chain we had created and call Rosie, who would then call Julie.

Suzanne stomped back into the front hall and stood practically in my face, absolutely fuming. Naturally that made me want to stay on the phone longer. Unfortunately, we have so many people in our family we have to have a telephone time limit.

"So, listen," I said, stretching out the end of my conversation with Becky, "pass the word on. This is so great!"

Suzanne was pacing up and down the hall by that time. "Allie, I mean it. Get off!" she whispered menacingly in my other ear.

"Gotta go, Beck," I said quickly, trying to suppress a giggle. "I'll call you later."

As soon as I hung up the phone rang again. That time it was for my ten-year-old brother, Mike. Suzanne let out her breath in a huff and ran up to her room. It's hard for me to have much sympathy for Suzanne. I mean, she's the oldest so she gets all kinds of privileges. She's also really cute and totally self-assured. Both she and her boyfriend, Tommy, treat me like a kid sister, and there are few things in this world worse than being treated like a kid sister. I suppose sometimes I treat my younger sister and brothers (Caroline, Mike, and Mouse, whose real name is Jonathan and who's four) like Suzanne treats me, but I try not to.

About an hour later Mrs. Jackson came by and handed me an envelope. I was really curious to know how much of a bonus was in there, but I didn't think it would be polite to look until after she left.

"There's something else I want to mention to you, Allie. Not only did my daughter go on and on about how wonderful the party was, but when she told me about the skating parade she also said that you sang that rainbow song just as well as Vermilion."

"Oh, no!" I blurted out, feeling uncomfortable. "I mean, she's my favorite singer, b-but I can't really sing like she does."

"I don't know, Allie. Patti's very interested in music and she really raved about your voice. I've never heard her do that before." She smiled at me. "She's a smart kid."

I didn't know what to say. I tried to find something fascinating to stare at in the living room drapes.

Mrs. Jackson touched my arm. "Listen, it just so happens that I'm the general manager of WCAN-TV. I don't know if you've heard about this, but we're sponsoring a talent contest for young teens. I think you should enter."

Unbelievable! It was spooky, hearing about the contest twice in one day. I cleared my throat, which suddenly felt as if a huge frog were living in there, croaking away. "Thanks for telling me about it, Mrs. Jackson."

"So you'll enter?" she asked me.

"Uh . . . I don't think so."

"Why not?"

I took a deep breath. "Well, mostly because I'd be too scared. The thing is, I c-can't really sing in front of people."

Mrs. Jackson looked very sympathetic. "I still think you should consider it. Here, I brought you an entry blank." She handed it to me. "Promise me you'll at least think about it?"

I stared at my sneakers. "I'll think about it," I whispered.

"Good," said Mrs. Jackson. "And thank you again for the wonderful party."

She turned to walk to her car, but then suddenly she looked back at me. "You know, Allie, today at the party you sang in front of a lot of people and you weren't nervous at all. I think maybe you forgot to be scared because they were children." She gave me a little wave and walked to her car.

Suddenly it didn't seem important how much money was in the envelope, or even that Suzanne was standing in the front hall screaming about the phone. Because Mrs. Jackson was right: when I was singing in front of kids I wasn't nervous or shy, and I never stuttered at all.

I sighed as I headed up to my room to face five pages of math homework. If only the whole world were populated by eight-year-olds, I could be a really big star!

Three

Becky and I were in the cafeteria line at lunch the next day. I peered into the vat of unidentifiable brown gunk called the Hot Lunch Special.

"What do you suppose that is?" I asked Becky.

"I think it began life as meat loaf," Becky giggled. We skipped the special and took containers of yogurt and tuna-fish sandwiches, then sat down at our usual table. Julie had arrived before us and was happily chowing down on the infamous Hot Lunch Special.

Becky made a face at Julie. "How can you eat that?"

Julie looked down at the lumpy glop. "Actually, it tastes a lot better than it looks. It's no competition for the Moondance's cuisine, though, so I think your parents' restaurant will stay in business." Julie polished off the last of the ex-meat loaf and started in on her chocolate cake. She is one of those people who can eat and eat and never gain any weight. She also eats just about anything. Some of her food combinations amaze me. For example, she loves anchovies *and* pineapple on the same pizza.

"Hi, Rosie," Becky said as Rosie slid her tray onto the table. "Good. Now that we're all here, I wanted to tell you that I got a call last night asking us if we'd do a birthday party for Aline Rose's five-year-old sister, Sharon."

Rosie looked at me mischievously, ignoring Becky. "So, is Dylan cute or what?" she said, as she opened her milk.

I bit into my tuna-fish sandwich and tried to look casual. The secret truth was, I had had sort of a crush on Dylan Matthews ever since I ran into him in the mall. I hadn't told anyone, not even Becky, but lately Rosie had been giving me looks that made me wonder if she suspected.

Becky laughed. "I don't believe you, Rosie. Not even a 'Hi, how are you?', just 'Is Dylan cute or what?' "

Rosie shrugged and sipped her milk. "I believe in hitting the important topics first."

"He's some kind of science whiz," Julie said as she started in on her second piece of chocolate cake. "I heard he was the only one who got a hundred on the frog anatomy quiz."

Becky made a face. "Ugh, frog dissection. That

was so gross. I swear, the next time Russell puts frogs' legs on the menu at the Moondance, I'm eating at the mall."

"It's no wonder he did so well on the quiz," said Julie. "His mother's a biology professor at Taylor College."

"How do you know so much about him?" I asked Julie.

"Mark Harris is friends with him, and Mark kind of told me about him."

Rosie raised her eyebrows. "When did this happen?"

"When he walked me to English class this morning," Julie said nonchalantly.

"No lie?" Rosie shrieked. "Mark walked you to class? In front of everyone?"

Julie really liked Mark and I could tell how happy she was, but she didn't want to make it into a big deal. "His class was in the same direction as mine was, that's all." She eyed the apple on Rosie's tray. "Are you going to eat that?"

"Be my guest," Rosie offered. She swiveled back around to face me, put her elbow on the table, and leaned her chin on her hand. "Well, if you ask me, Dylan is a major hunk."

Becky snorted. "If we ask you, Godzilla is a major hunk. Now, can we talk about something really important, such as the party for Sharon Rose?"

"Oh, we can deal with that later. Let's talk about something *else* really important, such as getting Allie to enter that talent competition," said Rosie.

"I agree," said Julie between bites of the apple. She looked at me. "I wish I could sing. It would be so cool. I know what I'd do—I'd enter 'Star Search'!"

"What a great idea!" said Becky. "Allie, you're better than a lot of the singers I've heard on that show."

"Oh, come on, you guys," I said.

"It's true," Rosie said, finishing off her sandwich.

Julie laughed. "Like I always say, if you've got it, flaunt it."

"I wish you would just forget about it," I said quietly.

Becky sighed. "Isn't there some way we can convince you?"

I shook my head. "Really, Beck, I can't—" But before I could finish explaining why I couldn't enter, who should stroll over to our table but Mark Harris and Dylan Matthews!

"Hey," said Mark, but he was looking at Julie. Julie quickly swallowed the bite of apple that was in her mouth and put the uneaten half down on her tray. She just seems to be getting more and more self-conscious around boys. For a while after she first got braces on her teeth she was so upset with how she looked that she vowed never to eat in public again. That didn't last too long, or at least around us, but I guess she still worried that food might get stuck in her braces or something and she'd look gross. I knew how it felt to be self-conscious so I couldn't really blame her.

"Was that bio quiz a killer or what?" Mark asked.

Becky shook her head. "I hate those surprise quizzes of hers! It really doesn't seem fair."

Mark grinned. "Remember how Casey got kicked out of Ms. Pernell's class for switching his dead frog with a live one? Well, he told me that when Ms. Pernell made him stay after school to make up the dissection work, his frog's eyeball flew across the room and landed on her glasses."

We all started laughing. "I don't believe it!" Rosie said.

"I believe it," said Mark, grinning.

Julie shook her head. "I'd vote him Most Likely to Commit a Major Felony."

Mark shifted his book to his other arm. "He may be my cousin, but you can bet I'm never studying for bio with him again. Now, if I knew science like

Dylan here, I'd be home free. I wouldn't have to study at all."

"Hey, Harris, I study," Dylan protested.

Mark snorted. "Yeah, right." He looked at Julie. "This guy speed-reads college textbooks for fun."

Before she remembered her braces, Julie smiled. She quickly covered her mouth with her hand.

Dylan shook his head at Mark and looked over at me. "How did you do on the quiz, Allie?"

I was startled that he asked me in particular. I hadn't even thought he remembered my name. "Okay, I g-guess," I stuttered. I hated the way I sounded, like some stupid airhead! "I'm not very good at science," I added lamely.

Becky laughed. "Allie's got to be the most modest person on earth. She gets good grades in everything. But actually, her claim to fame is singing."

Dylan's face brightened. "Oh, yeah? My older sister, Megan, is a vocal music major at Taylor College. I think it's great to be able to sing."

"See?" said Rosie, staring at me.

"See what?" I asked.

"Everyone thinks it's great to be able to sing. I mean, what good is it to have such a terrific voice if you don't let people hear it?" Rosie asked me.

"We're trying to convince Allie to enter the talent competition that WCAN-TV is sponsoring," Julie explained to Mark and Dylan.

"You should do it." Dylan smiled at me.

I didn't want to have to explain to this guy with the beautiful blue eyes that I was scared to death to sing in public. Fortunately, I was literally saved by the bell. I never thought I'd be so happy to see lunch end.

We all gathered up our books and headed out of the cafeteria.

"So, do you think you'll enter the competition?" Dylan asked me on the way out the door.

I shrugged and tried to act casual. "I don't know. I don't think I have enough time."

"I guess you're busy practicing for the glee club concert," Dylan said.

The school glee club was rehearsing for a concert of music from Broadway shows. Naturally, Dylan assumed I was in the glee club. How could I possibly admit that I was too chicken even to try out for it?

"Actually, I'm really busy with Party Line stuff," I said slowly. I was willing myself not to stutter in front of Dylan.

"Oh, yeah," said Dylan. "I heard about that. You guys run a party business, right?" I nodded at him as we walked down the hall. "I think that's great. You must make a lot of money. Well, anyway, I'd like to hear you sing some time," he added after a pause. "Catch you later." Dylan walked off toward his next class.

Was it my imagination, or did he sort of like me? My heart must have stopped for a second because all of a sudden I felt it thumping loudly in my chest.

Becky watched me watch Dylan walk down the hall. "You like him!" Becky said. She fixed her eyes right on my face. I couldn't tell whether she was mad or amused.

I turned away quickly. "I do not. I don't even know him," I said.

"Mm-hmm," was all she said.

The one-minute bell rang and Becky headed upstairs. "See you after school," she called out. We had arranged to meet Rosie and Julie and walk home so that we could spend some time planning Sharon Rose's party.

All afternoon I thought about what Rosie had said, that I should let people hear my voice. I wondered whether my friends might just be saying I was a really good singer because they wanted to be nice. Sometimes I thought I really had talent, but other times I didn't feel like my singing was very special at all. *Oh well,* I thought, *if I can't open my mouth in front of anyone older than eight, I'll never know anyway.*

What kept bothering me, though, was that deep down I felt that I was quitting before I'd even tried. I hated that feeling. I knew Vermilion wasn't a quitter, and she'd told me not to be one, either. I sighed. Why was everything so complicated?

Finally it came to me. I would ask our music teacher, Ms. Thomason. She's also the glee club director. Ms. Thomason is incredibly cool. She actually appeared in two Broadway shows in New York City before she decided the city wasn't for her and moved to Canfield. She is the absolute star of the Canfield Civic Theater and plays most of the leads in the musicals they put on. I had seen her play Eliza Doolittle in *My Fair Lady* and Anna in *The King and I*. If she said I really had talent and I should enter, then I would try, even if it meant having to face people and maybe stutter in front of them. That thought scared me to death, and I half hoped she'd tell me not to waste my time.

When school got out I summoned up all my courage and went to the music room. Ms. Thomason was sitting at the piano, practicing.

I was so nervous, my palms were sweating. "Um, excuse me, Ms. Thomason. C-could I speak with you a minute?"

She smiled and put away the sheet music.

I took a deep breath. One reason that I felt a little ridiculous talking to Ms. Thomason about the contest was that I'd talked to her a long time ago about maybe joining the glee club. But then I never joined. She'd never said anything to me about it, so I don't know if she minded or not. I minded, though. It made me feel silly.

"Well, the thing is, I wanted to talk to you about the WCAN talent competition." Just that day in music class Ms. Thomason had mentioned the contest and encouraged students to enter. Everyone in class had turned around to look at Marsha Clark, who got all the solos in glee club. Marsha's friends all started telling her she should enter. Becky, Julie, and Rosie had stared at me, but I had just looked down at my desk.

"Yes," said Ms. Thomason. "Would you like to enter?"

I bit my lower lip and made myself get the words out. "I don't know. I mean, what I want to know is, if you really think I have any t-talent."

"Listen, Allie, I'll tell you what I really think. I would encourage any student to enter, because I think it could be a good learning experience."

I had a sick feeling in my stomach. As Becky would say, you know you're in trouble as soon as an adult uses the term "learning experience." I was sure that was Ms. Thomason's nice way of telling me my voice wasn't any good after all.

"Thanks for telling me the truth," I mumbled, picking up my book bag.

"The truth? Why, Allie, I haven't said anything about you yet! Sit down, please." I sat in the front row and Ms. Thomason sat down next to me, leaning toward me as she spoke. "What I am saying is that I would encourage any of my students to try, but you, Allie, you I will implore to try. You have a special gift," she said simply.

Me? A special gift? I didn't even know Ms. Thomason had ever noticed my singing at all! Automatically, I started to protest. "Oh, no, I—" but Ms. Thomason cut me off.

"You see? That's what you always do. You're very self-deprecating." I must have looked puzzled, because she added, "I mean that you always undervalue your talents and skills."

"It's just that . . . I don't feel confident, I guess."

"Yes, I understand that," said Ms. Thomason. "But I would love to have your voice in the glee club, and I'd love to convince you of how talented you are."

"Me?" I asked her.

"You!" said Ms. Thomason, with a laugh. "I suppose you think I don't know how good you are because I don't give you solos in class, but I do.

The problem is, *you* don't know, and until you do no one can prove it to you."

"I feel so self-conscious," I managed.

Ms. Thomason nodded. "I know. You sort of want to enter that contest and win, and you sort of don't want to. Am I right?"

I looked at the floor and nodded.

"Right," she said briskly. "It isn't a bad thing to be modest, but sometimes being too modest can prevent you from doing the things you really want to do. Tell you what—if you're willing to work hard and make a serious commitment, I'm willing to help you. What do you say?"

I looked up at her expectant face. "Yes!" I blurted out, before I even realized I was saying it.

Ms. Thomason reached over and squeezed my hand. "I'm so glad! We'll need to work together after school and also on weekends for the next couple of weeks. Are you ready to put that kind of time into this?"

"Yes, I think so," I said solemnly.

"And will you be able to meet with me this Saturday—no, I mean Sunday. I can't make it Saturday. Can we get together on Sunday after lunch?"

"Uh-huh," I mumbled. I was beginning to get rattled again, and my voice shook a little. Ms. Thomason heard it and smiled at me warmly.

"I know it's scary, Allie. Most new challenges

are. But it doesn't mean nearly as much when something comes easily to you." I nodded in agreement.

"Good," she said. "Now, first things first. We've got to pick your music. Do you have something in mind?"

"I don't know what would be right for this kind of competition," I said.

Ms. Thomason stood up and walked around the room as she talked. She seemed really excited about working with me. "Okay, then, tomorrow we'll start right after school. I'll bring in a selection of sheet music and we'll see what works best for you. Off the top of my head, I'd say a ballad, something melodic with a wide range." She stopped and looked at me with a smile on her face. "You do have a wonderfully wide range. Do you know what that means?"

I shook my head no.

"It means that you can handle both the high notes and the low notes equally well," Ms. Thomason explained. "So I say we show off your range. How does that sound?"

"It sounds okay," I said tentatively.

Ms. Thomason peered at my face. "Are you a little worried about what you're getting yourself into?"

"Yes," I meekly admitted.

"Well, good. That just proves you take this seriously. I think you'll do just fine," she added.

I stood up and hugged my book bag to my chest. "Thanks a lot for helping me, Ms. Thomason."

She smiled a beautiful smile. "My pleasure, Allie."

I practically ran to the side entrance where Becky, Rosie, and Julie were waiting so we could walk home together. They were sitting on the steps and were in the middle of a discussion about Sharon Rose's birthday party.

"What took you so long?" asked Becky.

"Sorry. I stopped to talk with Ms. Thomason about the talent contest."

Their faces lit up. They stared at me expectantly.

"And?" said Rosie.

"And—I'm going to do it! She's going to help me! Isn't that fabulous?" I blurted out.

All three of them screamed and hugged me at once.

"How do you feel?" asked Becky.

"I'm really excited, and also really scared," I admitted.

"You'll be great!" Rosie cried.

Julie rolled up her copy of *Saucy* and pretended it was a microphone. "Ladies and gentlemen, please welcome to our stage the one, the only—

Allie!" She turned to me and spoke in her normal voice. "Really big stars only need one name."

"You guys are crazy," I said, laughing.

We kidded around the rest of the way home, and before we knew it we were in front of the Moondance Café.

"Oh, rats," said Becky. "We didn't get much planning done for the party. Well, we can talk about it on the bus tomorrow. And don't forget about the Party Line meeting. Sunday at one o'clock in my attic, as usual."

"Oops," I said in a little voice. "I goofed up. I have to work on my music with Ms. Thomason, but because she can't make it on Saturday we had to schedule it for early Sunday afternoon. Could we make our meeting a little later?"

They all agreed we could. As Julie put it, "For the next Vermilion, I guess we can change our plans a little."

I couldn't help letting my outside show how I felt inside, and so for the rest of the day I walked around with a huge grin on my face. I bet I even fell asleep grinning.

Four

During the next two weeks time just seemed to fly by. I worked with Ms. Thomason after school twice a week and on Sunday. The song we decided on for me to sing was "Over the Rainbow." Ms. Thomason explained that it would show off my wide vocal range; she thought that would impress the judges. She also said that I had a very sweet, pure-sounding voice, which would work well with that song. Still, she told me, it was a difficult song, particularly for someone with an untrained voice (like me), and I'd have to work really hard to do the song well. I'd have to learn to breathe like a singer, taking good, deep breaths so that I could sing an entire line without gasping for air, and also so my notes would sound full and rich. I learned, too, about something called placement, which means where you feel the vibrations in your head and chest when you sing a note. It all sounded kind of overwhelming, but I knew I loved the song and I trusted Ms. Thomason's judgment. I had thought about doing a Vermilion song, but Ms. Thomason pointed out that most of her songs would sound better with a whole band instead of just a piano for accompaniment.

At one of our rehearsals Ms. Thomason explained to me what the preliminary competition would be like. She said that the fifty contestants who had signed up would be divided arbitrarily into two different groups of twenty-five each. Both preliminary rounds would be held at the mall in front of a panel of judges, including the conductor of the Canfield College Orchestra, executives from WCAN-TV, and the principal of Canfield High. From the original fifty contestants, twenty would be chosen for the semifinals; after that, five would be chosen as finalists. There wouldn't officially be an audience until the final competition, when a show for the public would be put on at the Canfield Civic Center. I couldn't possibly imagine me having anything to do with that final competition. I figured I'd be happy if I could make it through the preliminaries and not fall on my face.

The Friday night before the preliminaries I was so nervous I couldn't sleep. I just lay there hugging my pillow and picturing myself up there stuttering in front of all those judges. When I finally fell asleep I had a horrible nightmare that I went up on stage, opened my mouth, and—no sound came out. Nothing!

The next morning I was lying awake in bed imagining all the things that could go wrong when my mom came into my room looking all happy and excited. "Hey, today's the day," she said with a smile. "Becky's on the phone."

I looked at the clock next to my bed. It was 8:15. I shook my head and looked at my mom incredulously.

She laughed. "I know," she said. "I couldn't believe Becky would be up this early, either."

I ran to get the phone.

"Becky?"

"Hi! I just called to say break a leg. That's show biz talk, you know," she said with a laugh.

"I can't believe today's the preliminary! I have about a million things to do," I said.

"Well, don't let me keep you. Are you sure you won't change your mind and let me come hear you?" she asked.

"I'm sure," I said. "I wouldn't want you to see me flop."

"Quit thinking like that!" Becky ordered. "Anyway, call me as soon as you know the results." I promised I would and hung up the phone.

I raced through my shower—for once the entire family gave me first crack at the bathroom—and then stared at my face in the bathroom mirror. I looked pale. And scared. I rummaged in the medicine cabinet for Suzanne's brown mascara and put a touch on my eyelashes. Then I used a little of her pink blush and lip gloss. I surveyed the results. *Well, at least I don't look like a ghost anymore,* I said to myself.

Hanging on my closet door was the outfit that Rosie had picked out for me to wear. It was bright red, and when she had suggested it to me I told her I wasn't sure it was right. Then Rosie told me she'd read in the newspaper that when reporters wore red—scarves, ties, shirts, whatever—to a news conference, they got picked more often to ask their questions. Rosie said that if I wanted to get noticed, I should wear red.

Deep down inside, I really did want to be noticed. I put on the red skirt and sweater, then stood in front of the mirror to brush my long, wavy brown hair. My mom came in carrying a red velvet ribbon. "I'm so proud of you for doing this, Allie."

"I haven't done anything yet," I reminded her.

"Just entering is a big step," my mom said as she helped me adjust the ribbon. "There. You look beautiful."

I gave her a kiss, grabbed my sheet music, and

rushed out the door to meet Ms. Thomason at the mall.

Overnight, one section of the mall had been turned into a small theater. At both ends of the stage were large signs that read, WCAN-TV Talent Search for Young People. Next to them were smaller signs that read, Preliminary Competition. A table for the judges was set up right below the stage, with forms and pencils in front of every seat. Behind that were twenty-five chairs, each marked with a number, where all the contestants would sit. Ms. Thomason had explained to me that the second group of twenty-five preliminary contestants, including Marsha Clark from my school, would perform that evening. For the preliminaries I would be able to sit in the audience and watch the other contestants, but if I made it to the semifinals, I'd have to wait backstage.

I pushed through the blue velvet curtains behind the stage and found a huge crowd of people backstage. Most of them seemed to be laughing or singing or screaming. Two clowns were juggling bowling pins and one girl was standing on her head. I made my way past a tall kid in a tuxedo practicing his tap-dance routine and a girl in a bright pink leotard who kept trying to practice dance steps while her mother curled her hair with a curling iron. I stopped for a moment to watch a girl in a dramatic black dress rehearse a scene from a play in which her character apparently died at the end. At least I *think* her character died, because the girl clutched her throat, slowly sank to the floor, and let out a final cough. It was fascinating.

I was startled by a loud voice calling out over the din, "Registrants! All registrants see me!" I looked around to see who the voice belonged to and spotted the skinniest woman I had ever seen, wearing a dress the color of lime popsicles. (I knew Rosie would call that dress a total fashion mistake.) The woman was holding a clipboard and looked harried.

"Name?" she said to me, pencil poised above her clipboard.

"Allison Gray."

She checked my name off on her list. "Allison, you will go on fifteenth. Remember that number. You're right after Rex, the Klutzy Magician."

I wasn't sure I had heard her correctly.

"Excuse me, did you say 'Rex, the Klutzy Magician'?"

She rolled her eyes. "Exactly." I felt bad for Rex already.

A tall, gangly guy with freckles ran over to us. Over his tuxedo he wore a black cape with scarlet lining. His carrot-colored hair stood up all over his head.

"Did you just call my name? Rex, the Klutzy Magician?"

The thin woman had a pained look on her face. "I already registered you, Rex."

"I know that, but I just heard my name again," he explained.

"I was just telling this young lady that she's on after you, that's all." The woman looked over our heads and walked away yelling, "Registrants! All registrants see me!"

A button fell off of Rex's cuff and he elbowed me in the side as he bent over to retrieve it.

"Oh, sorry." His face turned all red. "I'm Rex," he added.

"Allie," I said.

He dropped the button in his pocket and ran his hands through his hair. It looked even messier than it had before.

"The truth is, I'm really nervous," Rex confided. "I haven't had a lot of practice doing my magic act yet."

I managed a smile. "I'm sure you'll do fine."

His face lit up. "You think so?"

Actually I didn't think so at all. I figured a good magician had to have some coordination, but here was a boy who was a hundred times more klutzy than Becky.

"Want to see my big opening?" he asked hopefully.

"Rex, I'd like to, but I have to find my music teacher. Good luck," I added, and went off in search of Ms. Thomason.

I finally spied her in the crowd and made my way over to her.

"Hi, Allie. You look spectacular! Let's try to find someplace reasonably quiet to get you warmed up. I thought they'd have a piano back here, but they don't, so we'll have to use a pitch pipe," she said as we made our way through the mass of people. Finally we found a free space a bit away from the crowd.

"Now remember, Allie, how we practiced breathing." Ms. Thomason rummaged through her large bag to find the pitch pipe.

I looked around while Ms. Thomason was searching. To my left was a large group of giggling girls standing near the rear steps to the stage. They all seemed to be surrounding one person. Finally the group parted and I saw who was the center of their attention.

The girl was beautiful. She was about fourteen or fifteen, with long, straight, perfect blond hair that fell over one eye. She was wearing an all-white outfit that looked expensive even from all the way across the room. Around her neck she wore pearls that looked just like the ones my father gave my mother for their anniversary. The girl glanced at me, and suddenly I felt like a stupid, ugly kid in my red velvet hair ribbon. She leaned over and whispered something to her friends. They all turned around to look at me and giggled. The girl smiled triumphantly and tossed her perfect blond hair.

"Ah, here it is." Ms. Thomason held up the pitch pipe. She played a tone for me to match. I turned my back on the snobby girls and concentrated on warming up my voice. First I sang scales, which are sequences of eight notes in a row on one breath. The scales went higher and higher. Then we did arpeggios, which are patterns of four notes up and four notes down. While I practiced I vowed not to let those girls bother me, and told myself I didn't care what they thought. I could hear my voice quavering, though, and I knew it was from more than just normal nerves. I was letting myself get all shaken up at the thought of performing in front of people who might not like me or my songs.

Finally the thin woman with the clipboard called for attention. She had to raise her voice above the din three times before everyone finally quieted down.

"My name is Bonnie Rappitz, from WCAN-TV, and I will be the emcee for today's round of preliminaries." Bonnie Rappitz? That was her name? I stifled a giggle and so did some other kids. Her name sounded a lot like *bunny rabbits*, and I wondered whether her parents had realized what it sounded like. "When you take your seats," Ms. Rappitz continued, "sit in the order in which you will be performing. You'll find all the chairs clearly marked with a number. Does anyone have any questions?" she asked.

The girl who had been practicing her dance steps raised her hand meekly. Her face looked kind of green. "Where's the bathroom?" she whispered. Ms. Rappitz pointed and the girl ran toward the door, her mother trailing after her. Looking down at her clipboard again, Ms. Rappitz's nose twitched as she pursed her lips. I couldn't help giggling a little. I felt sort of like Alice in Wonderland—I thought she might actually turn into a rabbit before my very eyes!

"Now, there's no need to be nervous!" Ms. Rappitz announced in her shrill voice. "The judges are your friends. So, good luck, everybody!"

Ms. Thomason gave me a little hug. "Good luck, Allie. Just remember, breathe deeply and concentrate!" she said. I tried to smile back at her but my lips were already starting to quiver. She lifted my chin and looked at me. "Here's the best advice I can give you," she said, looking me straight in the eye. "In the theater they call it 'acting as if.' Get up there and act as if you believe that you are the most fantastic singer in the whole world. Who knows? One day, it might even be true."

I walked out and found my seat, number fifteen, right next to Rex, the Klutzy Magician. As I sat down next to Rex, the beautiful blond-haired girl walked by me and said under her breath, but loud enough so that I could hear, "Well, if it isn't Little Red Riding Hood." I felt myself blushing the same color as my outfit. I wished I had worn white, like her. I wished I could have run away and hid. I wished I were any place except right there, waiting to sing and looking like Little Red Riding Hood.

You've got to get hold of yourself, I told myself firmly. *What do you think other people would do?* I thought about Suzanne. I knew what she'd say: "She's just trying to psych you out, Allie! Forget her!" I smiled a little. Then I imagined Rosie saying, "Excuse me, but white wool with pearls? My grandmother wore that to my mother's wedding twenty years ago!" I actually laughed out loud at that one. Finally I remembered Ms. Thomason telling me to "act as if." I sat up a little straighter in my chair. No matter what happened, I knew I wasn't going up on that stage alone.

The talent show started, and some of the kids were really good. (I kept getting distracted by the guy sitting next to me, though. Rex, the Klutzy Magician, kept getting his cape stuck under his chair legs. Once he moved the chair leg and put it back down on his own foot.) There was a really good dancer, a girl named Elizabeth who was a freshman at Canfield High. She did a ballet to Beethoven's "Moonlight Sonata" and wore a gauzy white dress.

Number ten was a girl with the reddest hair and the most freckles I'd ever seen in my life. Ms. Rappitz introduced her. "Our next contestant is Belinda Kessler. Belinda is a seventh grader at Sayville Middle School. She will sing 'Whistle a Happy Tune' from the musical *The King and I*."

Belinda had the loudest voice I'd ever heard in my life. The problem was, Belinda seemed to be tone-deaf. She just picked out any note and boomed it out, making up her own melody that didn't sound much like "Whistle a Happy Tune." I remembered Ms. Thomason saying she would encourage any student to enter the contest, no matter how talented (or untalented) he or she was, but all I could think was that it would have been a big favor to give this girl a clue and steer her toward nuclear science or brain surgery or just about anything other than music. With the second verse, Belinda added a little bad tap dancing. She tippy-tapped around the stage, illustrating the song's lyrics with wild arm gestures.

In the middle of "Whistle a Happy Tune," there's a part where the singer is actually supposed to whistle a couple of lines. Evidently Belinda couldn't whistle, because she whipped out a kazoo and played the two lines, still continuing her tap dancing as best she could. Her big finish involved falling to her knees and spreading out her arms as she boomed the final out-of-tune note. Rex leaned over to me. "That's my girlfriend," he said with great pride. I wanted to laugh, but I could hear the blond-haired girl's friends howling and whispering how totally stupid Belinda was. Suddenly I didn't feel so much like laughing anymore.

Finally Ms. Rappitz introduced number fourteen: Rex, the Klutzy Magician. I wished him good luck in a whisper and he smiled at me before tripping over his own feet. He made his way up to the stage and began his act. He showed the audience a top hat, and let us see there was nothing inside it. He said he would be pulling a rabbit out of the hat. He asked a judge to say the magic words, and presto—instead of pulling a rabbit out of his hat, his pants fell down, revealing baggy clown pants with rabbits printed all over them. It was a riot! Next he went to smell the flower in his lapel, but squirted himself in the eye by mistake. He got the idea of having someone else smell the flower so he could squirt them, but the flower squirted backward and got him again. Every time one of his tricks backfired, he acted as if he were really embarrassed. At the end of his act he took out his handkerchief to cry because everything had gone wrong, but the handkerchief kept growing and growing. When he got a member of the audience to pull on the handkerchief, it finally came to an end—but the baggy clown pants were attached to the end!

The judges and the other contestants were still chuckling as he left the stage. Rex had turned out to be really funny, and I made a mental note to tell my friends about him. Maybe we could use him at one of our parties!

The next thing I knew, Ms. Rappitz was introducing me. Rex had returned to his seat next to me, his face flushed with success. "Go get 'em!" he said as I walked toward the stage. I felt as if I couldn't breathe at all, and I could feel my whole body trembling. I didn't even know if I could stand up! I felt a terrible panic come over me. But once I got up on the stage and saw Ms. Thomason's smiling face nodding encouragement to me from behind the piano, some confidence returned. I took a deep breath from way down in my chest, and nodded at her to start the accompaniment.

Somewhere over the rainbow, way up high
There's a land that I've heard of once in
a lullabye.

I tried to remember all the things I had worked on with Ms. Thomason, like good breathing and clear diction. When I finished the song I could see the judges nodding and smiling, but I assumed that they nodded and smiled at everyone.

I went back to my seat and collapsed. Rex whispered, "You were terrific!" I smiled at him with gratitude.

A few minutes later the girl with the blond hair got up to perform. Miss Rappitz introduced her.

"Next we have Laurie Sweet. She is a freshman at Canfield High, and she will be singing 'Gotta Talk to You Before I Go.'"

Laurie Sweet didn't have an adult on the piano accompanying her; she had a gorgeous guy playing electric guitar. And who was the gorgeous guy? The very same guy I had practically knocked over at the roller rink!

I could tell that Laurie felt really confident about her singing, and she had a great voice. She whipped her blond hair back over her shoulders and danced around as she sang, smiling at the judges the whole time. When she got to the end of the second verse she danced around some more, then played air guitar for a second, just like singers do on MTV. Then she actually winked at the judges! I couldn't believe it. I didn't think we were allowed to wink at the judges! She did a complicated spin perfectly and went back to singing the repeat of the refrain.

When she finished her friends whistled and applauded, even though an announcement had been made at the beginning of the judging that officially there was not supposed to be an audience at that level of the competition and therefore no one was supposed to applaud. When Laurie walked by me on her way back to her seat, she whipped her hair back over her shoulders and gave me a frosty look. I fantasized about her tripping over Rex's cape and landing on her superior butt, and had to bury my face in my hands to keep from laughing out loud.

When everyone had performed I made my way backstage and found Ms. Thomason. "You were wonderful!" she said, giving me a hug. I felt so happy! It was the first time I had sung in front of anyone besides my friends and young kids, and I hadn't stuttered or anything!

"I *really* want to thank you for helping me," I said, feeling suddenly shy again. Then I remembered I had left my sheet music on my chair. I told Ms. Thomason I had to go get it.

I rounded the corner fast and *bam!*—Rex, the Klutzy Magician, banged into me, dropping his magic tricks all over the floor.

"Oh—gee—oh, I'm sorry," Rex stammered. He bent over to retrieve his stuff and various things fell out of his pocket. "Oh, gosh, this always happens," he mumbled.

"Look, it's okay. I'll help you," I said. We started picking up Rex's stuff, scrambling between people's legs as they walked by. Someone else knelt down to help, and I glanced up to see who was being so thoughtful. It was the handsome guitar player! He stood up just as I did, both of us handing Rex his magic cards.

"I remember you!" he said when he saw me.

Oh, great, I thought. *He remembers me as the idiot from the roller rink parking lot.*

"You have a really great voice!" he said to me.

I could hardly speak. "Th-thanks."

Just then Laurie came over to us. "Jeff, they're

posting the names of the semifinalists. Let's go look." She gave me a cool look and started to drag Jeff off, but he turned his head around toward me and yelled, "Good luck!"

I got my sheet music, then headed for the crowd surrounding the list of semifinalists from my round of the preliminaries. My heart raced as I scanned the list. Laurie Sweet's name was there, of course. Rex, the Klutzy Magician, had made it, too. And . . . could it be? It was! There was my name—Allison Gray.

I twirled around and found Ms. Thomason reading over my shoulder. "I made it! I can't believe it!"

"You deserved to make it, Allie. I'm really proud of you. But this is only the beginning, you know. Are you ready to work harder than you've ever worked before?"

"Oh, absolutely," I gushed. "I'll work night and day."

"Well, we'll try to leave you time for little things, like eating and sleeping," she said with a smile.

But all I could think was, who needs to sleep? Who needs to eat? I, Allison Gray, was a semifinalist!

Five

Becky, Rosie, and Julie were laughing so hard they were practically crying. We were up in Becky's attic for our regular Sunday meeting, and I had just finished telling them about Rex, the Klutzy Magician, and the girl who played the kazoo to "Whistle a Happy Tune."

"That is so funny. We should hire Rex to entertain at Sharon Rose's party!" Becky cackled.

"Actually, it's not a bad idea to hire him for a party sometime," I said. "He's really a sweet guy. And funny! I think the little kids would love him."

"We could do a magic party sometime," Becky said thoughtfully. "The birthday kid could be the magician's assistant!" Becky looked over at Julie to tell her to write down the idea, since she's the secretary, but Julie had beat her to it. She waved her notebook in the air.

"Duly noted, Madam President," said Julie. Becky grinned at her.

"It is so cool that you made the semifinals, Allie," said Julie as she reached for the potato chips Becky had brought up for a snack.

Rosie stretched out and propped her head on a pillow. "And to think we talked you into trying out!"

"Well, thanks for believing I could do it," I said. "It really helped."

"Hey, I heard Marsha Clark didn't even make it to the semis," Rosie continued.

"Yeah. Ms. Thomason said she had a bad head cold yesterday. She tried, but I guess her voice sounded funny," I said. "I never got to hear her because she was in the other group."

"Less competition for you!" Becky laughed. "So, do we get to see you in the semifinals?" she went on.

"I would love to have you guys there," I said, "but Ms. Thomason said there's still not supposed to be an audience. The semis are being held somewhere at the TV station."

"Boo on that," Rosie said grumpily.

"Oh well," Becky said. "Your fan club will just have to wait until you reach the finals."

"Yeah, right," I snorted.

Julie threw a pillow at me. "Cut it out, Gray. You made it this far, didn't you?"

Rosie wrapped her scarf around her head and

spoke with a strange accent. "Rosie ze Gypsy sees you een ze finals! Rosie ze Gypsy sees all!"

I laughed and threw Julie's pillow at Rosie. "Great," I said. "Could Rosie the Gypsy possibly see the answers to Ms. Pernell's next bio quiz?"

Rosie continued in her gypsy character. "No, zis I cannot see. But I am getting a vision of a boy . . . no, not a boy, a hunk! Zis hunk sinks zat you are vunderful!"

"Oh?" I laughed. "And just who is this mysterious hunk?"

Rosie wiggled her eyebrows. "His name ees . . . Deelinn."

"I think your crystal ball needs to be cleaned," I said, reaching for a potato chip.

Rosie sat up and talked like a normal person. "Dylan Matthews, to be exact," she clarified. I was going to make another crack, but I looked at her face. She wasn't kidding!

"Get out of here!" I shrieked. "He doesn't even know who I am!"

"Wanna bet?" said Julie. "He told Mark you have a great smile."

"I do?" I blinked. "I mean, he did?"

Julie reached for the last potato chip. "No lie," she confirmed.

"Tell me exactly what he said," I demanded, "word for word."

Julie thought for a second. "Well, according to Mark, he said you were a really nice girl and you have a great smile."

I scrambled up, stood in front of the antique full-length mirror in the corner, and smiled at myself about six different ways. I didn't see what was so great about it.

"Um, excuse me," said Becky, sounding annoyed, "but we're supposed to be planning Sharon's party."

Becky was right, and I felt like an idiot standing there and smiling into the mirror. I sat back down and quickly changed the subject.

"We're doing fairy tales again, right?" I asked.

"Right," said Becky. "According to her mom, her favorite fairy tale is *Peter Pan*. I don't know if she'll want to come dressed as Peter or Wendy, though," she added.

"Let's think of some new games, because some of the kids who are coming were also at Lisette's fairy tale party," Julie pointed out.

"Good idea," I agreed.

"I've got it!" cried Becky. "A treasure hunt for Captain Hook's buried treasure!"

We started to plan the treasure hunt, but my mind wandered. Dylan Matthews liked me? What if I made the finals and he came to hear me sing? I couldn't sing in front of Dylan!

"Allie, what do you think?"

I was startled by Becky's voice, then embarrassed to realize I had daydreamed through the entire discussion.

"Well, um . . ."

Becky knew me too well and shook her finger at me. "You didn't hear a word of it, did you?"

I shook my head sheepishly.

"In that case, would the esteemed secretary please read the minutes back to the honorable vice president, who was daydreaming about how famous she's going to be?"

"I wasn't! I—"

"I'm *teasing* you, Allie. Honest." Becky smiled at me, and I was so relieved. I had thought she was really mad! I paid extra-close attention to the rest of the meeting, though.

We usually go together to buy the party supplies, but that week everyone was especially busy and so I was chosen to go pick up the supplies at The Perfect Party in the mall. I started toward home, thinking I'd detour to the mall on the way. But as I walked along I started thinking about the semifinals and about the voice lesson I'd had earlier that afternoon with Ms. Thomason.

She had told me that good singing was really acting on pitch. At first I wondered about that, since never in my wildest dreams had I thought I could be an actress. But when I thought about how Vermilion made me feel when she sang a song, I realized that she *was* acting, in a way. I wanted to be able to do that, too—to make people feel something when I sang.

I got so excited about practicing that I hurried straight home instead of stopping at The Perfect Party, figuring I could go out again later and pick up the supplies.

When I got home I raced up to my room and warmed up by doing scales. Then I started working on my song. By some miracle no one was home, so I could really lose myself in the music. I closed my eyes as I sang, and pictured myself flying—flying over the rainbow, toward some mysterious and wonderful land where all my dreams could come true.

It felt so wonderful to be singing like that! I didn't think about the book report that was due for English or my Party Line duties or any of the things I usually worried about. I just felt happy . . . and free.

Six

During the next week, I worked really hard with Ms. Thomason. One thing I found out is that becoming a great singer, or even a good one, is very hard work. Singers like Vermilion make it look so easy, but the more I learned the more I appreciated all the hard work it took. For example, I learned that there was a lot more to proper breathing than just taking a deep breath. Ms. Thomason had me lay down on the floor on my back, with a large magazine on the lower part of my stomach. She explained that if I breathed correctly from my diaphragm, which is a large muscle down there, when I inhaled the magazine should actually be pushed up into the air. At first when I tried this I couldn't make the magazine move at all. All that happened from my effort was that the next day my back and sides hurt! Ms. Thomason explained that I was developing muscles I had never used before, just like a long-distance swimmer or any other athlete. After a while I could lift the magazine a little, and then more and more. Once I learned to breathe correctly, I started doing it when I sang. The difference amazed me. I could sing twice as long without running out of air, and the notes sounded fuller and richer, too.

I got so excited about my singing lessons that it was hard to fit in everything else I was supposed to do. Normally Suzanne and I trade the chores we don't like to do—I do her babysitting and she does my dishwashing. But Suzanne got really mad at me because twice during that week she had to do all the dinner dishes *and* babysit for Mouse, too. I was even a day late with a book report for English, which is totally unlike me. Not only was I late, I'd only started the report the night before, and so it wasn't even very good.

I wished there were more hours in each day, and I vowed to try even harder to get everything done. I started making schedules and lists for each day, which helped a little. But to tell the absolute truth, it wasn't just the singing that was keeping me so busy and distracted. I also found myself thinking a lot about one particular, really cute guy—Dylan Matthews.

In biology that week we were studying the human skeletal system. As we sat in class on

Wednesday that week Ms. Pernell stood in front of a huge chart of the bones in the body, indicating each bone with her pointer.

"The human skeleton is a miraculous thing," she told us. "Each bone, down to the tiniest ones in your fingers, has a precise and perfect function." Ms. Pernell looked totally absorbed as she pointed out the humerus, clavicle, and maxilla—I guess she was as excited about bone stuff as I was about singing. Casey Wyatt clearly wasn't thrilled, however. He made fake snoring noises in the back of the room, and a bunch of kids could barely suppress their giggles. Ms. Pernell heard him and folded her arms across her chest.

"It would be wise to pay attention as we explore the bones in the leg, since you might just find yourself taking a pop quiz on this information any day now." She took off her glasses and glared right at Casey. Some kids around me groaned, and I looked back and made sure my notes were clear. I knew if Ms. Pernell said we "might" have a pop quiz, it was a sure thing.

I sneaked a look over at Dylan while Ms. Pernell was making her announcement. I was surprised to find him looking right back at me! I started to blush, but then he made a face about the pop quiz and I felt better. I smiled at him and he grinned. He had such a great smile.

When class got out I stopped at my locker to be sure I had all the books I needed for my homework. Becky's locker was right next to mine, and she started groaning about having to memorize the human skeleton.

"I mean, the entire human skeleton? Couldn't we just say we've got bones and call it a day?"

I laughed. "My dad taught me a good way to memorize," I told her. "It's called mnemonics. You take the first letter of each bone, for example, and make up a phrase that uses those letters. Then when you think of the phrase, it helps you remember the names of the bones." I opened our biology textbook to the diagram of the human leg. "Okay, this is the femur, patella, fibula, and tibia. That's F-P-F-T. Um . . . how about Funny People Feel Ticklish?"

"Or Foolish People Flunk Tests!" giggled Becky. "Hey, you're right. That really helps!"

Becky started making up funnier and funnier ways of remembering the bones.

"Frogs Play Fewer Trombones! Four Pigs Fear Tuna!"

Suddenly I felt a tap on my shoulder. I turned around, and there was Dylan Matthews.

"Hi, Allie. Listen, I missed yesterday's bio homework, and I was wondering if you had the notes." I had noticed he hadn't been in class the day before.

"Yeah, sure," I said, as nonchalantly as possible. As I flipped through my looseleaf to find the homework, I noticed that Becky had stopped laughing about our mnemonic phrases and seemed to find the inside of her locker totally fascinating.

"Here it is," I said, showing him my notebook. He leaned close to me to read the notes. I could see how blue his eyes were up close.

"Wow, you take neat notes," Dylan marveled. "No one can read mine."

"The notes aren't the hard part for me," I said. "It's remembering what's in them that's tough!"

"Thanks," said Dylan, handing me back my notebook. "You know, maybe we could study together for the quiz. I'm pretty good at science," he added casually.

He had asked me for a study date! I felt like turning cartwheels down the hall. Then I remembered that I always studied for biology with Becky, since science was her worst subject. I looked over at her but she still had her face buried in her locker. "I'd love t-to, b-but I'm already studying with B-Becky," I explained to Dylan. I was mortified to hear myself stuttering, and I hoped he hadn't noticed.

"Oh, well, maybe another time," Dylan said easily. "Hey, how's your singing going?"

"Okay," I said shyly, putting a few books into my locker.

"Like I said, maybe I can hear you sing sometime," Dylan said. "Anyway, thanks for letting me look at the homework. See you." He loped off down the hall. I looked after him, my heart racing a mile a minute.

I turned around and clutched Becky's arm. "Did you hear him? He asked me for a study date! You're my witness."

"I heard him," said Becky. She rummaged around in her locker some more. "I can't find that stupid birdhouse I was working on in shop class."

"A study date," I marveled, leaning against my locker.

"Ah, here it is!" Becky triumphantly pulled the birdhouse from the bottom of her locker. "You could have said you'd study with him, you know," Becky said, not looking at me. "I mean, I'm perfectly capable of studying on my own."

"No, I want to study with you," I said.

Becky laughed. "Allison Gray, that is a lie. As Julie's grandmother would say, you practically plotzed when he asked you." Julie's grandmother, Goldie, was always teaching her these great Yiddish expressions. I remembered that *to plotz* meant *to explode.*

I grinned at Becky. "Okay, you win. But it's the being asked part that's important, not the actual studying. Do you think he might like me?" I asked her hopefully.

"Of course he does. Everyone likes you, Allie. You are very likeable, okay? Now, can we go study or what?"

"Sure," I said. "Come on, I'll walk you home and we'll make up more unforgettable mnemonic phrases for the leg. How about Fifty Penguins Fry Tomatoes?"

At dinner that night I chattered on and on. I told my family about the talent competition, about school (okay, I guess I *did* mention Dylan's name a lot), and about Sharon Rose's party. As soon as the words were out of my mouth I gasped. I had completely forgotten to buy the supplies for Sharon's party! And *I* was supposed to be the organized one! I quickly got up from the dinner table and ran over to my notebook to make myself a note reminding me to pick up the supplies. *Close call,* I thought.

My mother looked concerned when I came back to the table. "What was that all about?"

"Just a note I needed to make to myself," I answered, sipping my milk.

My brother Mike reached for a roll. "If I made notes about stuff I was supposed to do, I'd just forget to look at the notes."

My father looked over at me. "Allie, do you think maybe you're pushing yourself a little too hard, what with the contest and school and The Party Line?"

"No, Dad, I'm fine. Honest." I smiled at my father to reassure him and picked up a chicken leg. The last thing I wanted was for my parents to decide I was too busy and make me cut back on my practice for the talent competition.

When we finished dinner I volunteered to do the dinner dishes. Suzanne looked at me as if I were crazy, because she knew I hated washing dishes, but I wanted to prove to my parents that I really did have time to do everything I was supposed to do. When I finished the dishes I went to call Becky.

"Hi, Beck, it's me."

"Oh, hi. I was just digging into my algebra homework. Thanks for the reprieve."

I told Becky how nervous I was getting about the semifinals. Becky reassured me. "Listen, the judges wouldn't have picked you as a semifinalist if you weren't good enough. They know talent when they hear it."

"Maybe they made a mistake," I ventured.

"And maybe they didn't," Becky replied.

"Yeah, maybe," I sighed.

"You'll be terrific. I just know it," said Becky. "Hey, I meant to tell you—I got another great idea for Sharon Rose's party. Crocodiles!" Becky exclaimed.

"Crocodiles?" I repeated doubtfully.

"Right! You know how Captain Hook always has trouble with crocodiles? Well, my brother told me he saw a five-foot-long inflatable crocodile at The Wishbone in the mall. I think we should get it. The kids'll love it!"

As soon as Becky started talking about Sharon Rose's party, I felt anxious and guilty, knowing I'd hardly given it any thought. The party was that Saturday and I hadn't even purchased the supplies yet.

I decided to change the subject. "Did you see Mark walking Julie to class again today?"

"Yeah. They look cute together," Becky said.

"Yeah. But I think Dylan's even cuter than Mark."

Becky laughed. "You would."

"What do you mean?" I asked innocently.

"Look, if you're going to start on the subject of boys, then I'd just as soon get back to my algebra."

"Are you mad at me for liking Dylan?" I asked her.

"Why should I be mad? He seems nice."

"Really nice!" I agreed.

"Right. Really, really nice. But algebra is calling to me."

"Okay, Beck, see you tomorrow."

I hung up, glad that Becky didn't mind that I liked Dylan. At least she said she didn't mind. Deep down I just wasn't so sure.

Seven

At last it was Friday, the day of the semifinals. Rosie told me to wear the same outfit I had worn for the preliminaries, but I was skeptical.

"Trust me," she said. "I read that when Barbra Streisand started out she always wore the same outfit to both the first audition and the callback." I figured if it was good enough for Barbra Streisand, it was good enough for me.

Right after school I went straight to the WCAN-TV offices. Registration was set up at a big desk in the front lobby. Ms. Rappitz sat behind the desk, checking off the names of the semifinalists as they arrived. This time she was wearing a shocking pink dress with large black exclamation points all over it. I knew Rosie would have rolled her eyes at that one. According to Rosie's Rules of Fashion, classics are best in the workplace. She always knows what will look right. Rosie is the one who figures out what we should wear for all

our parties. She says we should dress appropri-
ately for the particular party—but our clothes
have to be functional, too. For example, we all
wore jeans to the skating party. But when we gave
a dress-up party not long ago, we got dressed up,
too, so that we'd fit in. Of course, we couldn't wear
our best clothes, because with seven-year-olds you
never know when the ice cream is going to start
to fly!

I looked at Ms. Rappitz's outfit—she was defi-
nitely not wearing classics. I wondered if she
thought she should dress eccentrically because she
was in show business. She was frantically shuf-
fling papers and trying to listen to a young woman
whispering in her ear at the same time as she was
trying to register the semifinalists. And her nose
was still twitching like a rabbit's!

I checked in and then followed my routine of
warming up with Ms. Thomason. This time a
small room with a piano was provided for all the
singers to use for their warmups. We had each
been assigned ten minutes to use the room.

"Now remember, Allie, support the tone." I
knew that meant to breathe deeply and control
how fast I used up the breath as I sang the phrase.

I tried to focus all my attention on the warmups, but I was feeling a little sick to my stom-

ach. Before I knew it, my ten minutes were up and the next singer was waiting to use the room.

"Allie, I'm going to go phone my babysitter. My daughter has a bad cold and I just want to make sure everything's okay," said Ms. Thomason. She went off to find a phone, and I paced outside the rehearsal room, absolutely unable to sit still.

"Excuse me, is the rehearsal room free?"

I turned around and saw a smiling girl with curly brown hair. She looked to be a few years older than me.

"Yes, I'm done," I said.

"My voice teacher's late, but I thought I'd go in and warm up anyway. I'm so nervous!" Then she must have realized she hadn't introduced herself. "Oh, sorry, my name's Marci Berman. I'm so nervous, I'm just jabbering on."

"I'm nervous, too," I admitted. "My name's Allie Gray," I added shyly.

"Oh, I heard about you! You were in the first round of preliminaries, right? I was in the second, so that's why we haven't met. Laurie Sweet told me about you—I go to school with her."

She must have seen the change in my face, because she quickly reassured me, "Listen, she's been talking about you all week, and you're right if you think she didn't have anything nice to say. But take it as a compliment. If Laurie didn't consider you heavy competition, she wouldn't have mentioned you at all." She leaned closer to me. "Confidentially, she's a terrible snob. And she bleaches her hair."

Marci winked when she said that, so I didn't know if she was kidding or not, but I laughed and felt much better.

"Well, nice meeting you, Allie. Good luck!" she said, and went into the rehearsal room.

Ms. Thomason came back and we headed for the backstage waiting area just as Laurie Sweet showed up with Jeff, the cute guitar player.

She was dressed in a black leather miniskirt and a cropped black leather jacket. I had seen that outfit at Winter's and I knew it cost a fortune. I think Laurie saw me out of the corner of her eye, because she tossed her head and sighed theatrically. "I don't need to warm up," she said loudly to Jeff. "I wish they'd just hurry up." It seemed to me Jeff looked kind of disgusted with her, but maybe it was just wishful thinking on my part. Before she turned away, Laurie looked at me with surprise, as if she had just noticed me.

"Oh, hello. I've forgotten your name. . . ."

"It's Allie."

"Right. Allie. How sweet," she said, dripping sarcasm. "I didn't know you made the semis." She feigned great surprise, as if she thought the judges must have been sleeping or something.

"Well, I did." I was going to stand up to her and not stutter if it was the last thing I did. I looked her straight in the eye.

Just at that moment, Rex, the Klutzy Magician, showed up, dragging his magician's bag and tripping over his feet. He greeted me like a long-lost friend.

"Hi, Allie! You nervous? I'm nervous." He dropped his magician's bag on his foot and cracked his knuckles. A button popped off his shirt. He shook his head ruefully.

Laurie rolled her eyes and tossed her hair. "It figures you two would be friends." She smiled at me but her eyes looked like two hard marbles. "Good luck, Sally."

"Allie," I corrected her.

"Whatever." She took Jeff's arm and sauntered away.

Rex ran his hand through his hair. "She is not what I would call a very nice person," he reflected.

"That's an understatement," I said.

He picked up his magic bag and the handle broke off in his hand. He shook his head. "My mother says I'm an accident looking for a place to happen," he said sheepishly.

"Well, it seems to me you've turned a negative into a positive," I observed.

He cheered up immediately. "Hey, yeah, I guess you're right. Thanks!" He walked away mumbling, "A negative into a positive . . . yeah, that's it!"

Finally the contest started. I was so nervous, I paced endlessly back and forth. The first contestant was a classical pianist who played a Chopin waltz. From what I could tell, the pianist got all the notes right, but didn't seem to put a whole lot of emotion into his playing.

The second contestant was Laurie Sweet. (Talk about someone's last name not describing their personality!) I stood as near the back curtain as I could to hear her sing. Marci came up next to me to listen, too. We could hear Laurie count out loud to Jeff, as if he were an entire rock and roll band, "One, two, one-two-three-four!" Then Jeff started playing. Marci rolled her eyes and I stifled a giggle.

This time I listened more critically to Laurie's voice. Ms. Thomason had said I needed to develop a good ear, and that's what I was trying to do. When I listened carefully, I could tell that sometimes Laurie's high notes were forced and strident. I had learned a lot from Ms. Thomason about how to listen to music, and I realized that while

Laurie's voice might sound good to someone who wasn't listening closely, she didn't have the technique that made a good singer really good.

Before I knew it my number was called and I was up on the stage facing the judges. I thought it would be easier the second time, but once I saw those judges and heard my opening music, it was just as scary as ever.

I felt so scattered that when I started singing I wasn't even sure I had come in at the right place. I sang the first line very softly, but then I remembered Ms. Thomason had said, "Pick a spot in the back of the room and pretend there's someone standing there whom you'd love to be singing to." For some reason, I thought of my little brother, Mouse. I imagined him in that spot in the back of the room. His face was shining, and I was singing just for him.

Some day I'll wish upon a star
And wake up where the clouds are far behind me.
Where troubles melt like lemon drops
Away above the chimney tops,
That's where you'll find me!

Then something magical happened. I felt my voice soaring out of my chest. I felt the thrill of singing and the wonder of the words. It was everything I imagined singing in front of people could be. I didn't even think Vermilion could feel more than I felt singing "Over the Rainbow" and imagining my little brother, his eyes bright, in the back of the room.

I was in kind of a daze when I finished singing. I must have made my way offstage because the next thing I knew, a dancer was being introduced. A pianist followed the dancer, and then it was Rex's turn. This time I couldn't see his act, but I hoped he had developed a few new klutzy tricks to show the judges.

Finally, Marci went on. She sang "For Once in My Life" by Stevie Wonder, and she was terrific! Her voice was strong and beautiful. It seemed to me that her singing came from her heart, and not just from her vocal cords (like a certain bleached blond I could mention). Just like Ms. Thomason had explained to me, Marci was an actress when she sang the song. She was telling the audience how she felt, and she was really, truly feeling it. I was glad she was good, because she seemed like such a nice person.

After Marci had finished and the judges had started to confer, Ms. Thomason came backstage to see me.

"Allie, that was just beautiful," she exclaimed. For once, I felt in my heart that I really had done my best, so all I did was murmur, "Thank you." It felt great.

I knew that the finalists were going to be notified by phone that evening, but I tried to put it out of my mind. I told myself I had done my best and that was what counted. Still, I found myself going over every moment in my mind. Had I really sung well? Had I remembered to act the song and not just sing it? But as it got further away from the time I had performed, I could scarcely remember whether I had really been any good at all.

I was so nervous I couldn't swallow a bite of dinner. The phone rang at seven o'clock and my heart started hammering in my chest, but it was for Suzanne. My whole family stepped around me as if I were made of glass.

Mouse came up to me and patted my knee. "I bet you were the goodest, Allie." I hugged him hard, just as the phone rang again.

My mom came into the kitchen. "Allie, it's for you."

It's Becky, I said to myself. *I know it's Becky.* I picked up the phone.

"Hello?"

"Hello, is this Allison Gray?"

"Yes?"

"This is Mr. Kennedy from WCAN-TV. I'm very

pleased to tell you that you have been selected as a finalist in the talent competition. Congratulations!"

I almost screamed into the telephone, but I managed to speak in a reasonably normal voice. "Oh, thank you! Thank you so much!"

"You're very welcome. The finals are next Friday evening at the Canfield Civic Center. Someone from our staff will call you tomorrow and give you more details."

"Oh, yes, fine," I managed.

"Well, congratulations again. You were great!" said Mr. Kennedy.

After I hung up I couldn't control myself a second longer, and I raced into the living room screaming, "I made the finals! I made the finals!"

My mom and dad both hugged me at once, and my brothers and sisters ran into the living room. Everyone was so happy for me. "Oh, I've got to call Ms. Thomason. She'll be so happy. And I've got to practice!" I must have sounded alarmed, because everyone laughed as I ran off to call Ms. Thomason.

She was just as happy for me as I figured she'd be. "This is just fantastic, Allie. The finals are Friday evening, so we'll have to practice as much as we can during the week. We'll really need to work tomorrow afternoon and Sunday, too. Okay?"

Tomorrow afternoon? I had a gnawing feeling that there was something I was supposed to do on Saturday. I suddenly remembered what it was, and my stomach sank. Sharon Rose's party was the very next day! I hadn't remembered to buy the supplies, and on top of that, Ms. Thomason wanted to rehearse then! My heart beat like a jackhammer as my mind raced ahead for a possible solution. Could I get the supplies really early and still fit in a rehearsal before the party?

"Could it be very early Saturday?" I asked her hopefully.

"Sorry," she said, "but I've got plans with my family in the morning."

I gulped. "Okay, then. Saturday afternoon," I agreed.

"Fine. We'll work at my house at, say, one o'clock. See you then, Allie. I'm so excited for you!"

There was no way around it—I was about to let down my three best friends. This time I knew the phone chain wouldn't do. I would have to call each of them and explain that I had forgotten to buy the supplies for the party and that I couldn't even be there.

Calling Becky was the hardest of all. I dialed her number, almost wishing she wouldn't be home.

"Hello?"

It was her. "Hi, Becky. Guess what? I made the finals," I said.

She whooped into the phone. "Allie, I'm so proud of you!"

"Thanks," I said in a small voice. I felt sick to my stomach.

"What's wrong, Allie? You don't sound happy." It was just like Becky to notice.

"Oh, Becky, I feel terrible about this. I got so caught up in wondering whether I'd make the finals that I . . . I forgot to buy the stuff for Sharon Rose's party." I took a deep breath. "And I'm going to have to rehearse with Ms. Thomason tomorrow, so I won't be at the party."

Becky was quiet for a second. "Let me get this straight. You didn't get the party stuff and you're not going to be at the party?"

"Forgetting to get the supplies was totally my fault. I really don't want to miss Sharon's party, though, but tomorrow afternoon is the only time that Ms. Thomason could practice with me. Do you hate me?"

Becky sighed. "No, I don't hate you."

"I'll make this up to all three of you, I promise. Please tell me you understand."

"Well, I'm trying to understand, but it isn't easy," Becky grumbled. "I'm a little upset, because the party's going to be a lot more difficult to run with just the three of us."

"I know," I said, feeling miserable.

Becky was quiet for a second, then she said, "Look, I understand. I'm not too thrilled with the way things turned out, but I know how much this means to you—and I guess there isn't much you can do about Ms. Thomason's schedule."

I didn't say anything. I was really upset that I had disappointed my friends, and I was afraid my voice might crack.

"We'll be okay. We'll miss you, though," said Becky after a few seconds.

I swallowed hard. "I'll miss you, too."

Why couldn't I be in two places at once?

Eight

Monday afternoon Becky and I had made plans to meet at the side door of the school and walk home together. Julie and Rosie were staying for softball practice. When the final bell rang, I stopped by the music room before I went to meet Becky. When I got to the door, she was sitting on the steps, her chin in her hands.

"Sorry I'm late," I said breathlessly. "I had to run by the music room and pick up this book Ms. Thomason wants me to read. It's called *Power Singing*, and it looks really interesting. It's about how to focus your energy when you sing. Ms. Thomason told me that singing can be looked at as both an art and a sport, actually, since you have to develop the muscles and the physical control just the way an athlete does. It's all in this book." I held the book in front of Becky's face, but she just nodded and looked away.

"Are you okay?" I asked her.

"Sure. Why wouldn't I be?" she said.

Silence.

"Are you mad that I was late?" I asked her.

"No problem," she said, still looking away.

More silence. By that point we had left the school and gone an entire block, but Becky still wouldn't even look at me. I didn't know what to do. Finally I said, "So, how was Sharon Rose's party?"

"Fine," she said shortly. "Russell took me to get the supplies about an hour before the party," she added.

I bit my lower lip. "I would've gotten them when I remembered, but I knew the store was closed by then."

Becky didn't say anything and she *still* wouldn't look at me.

"I'll never let it happen again, Becky, I swear."

"Okay," she said, kicking a stick that was in her path.

I thought maybe I should change the subject. "I noticed Dylan was absent today," I said.

Becky stopped dead and turned to me. "There you go again!" she shouted. "I've absolutely had it!"

I looked at her, bewildered. "What?"

"All you ever talk about anymore is that stupid singing competition and that stupid guy!"

"That's not true!" I protested.

"It is true, so don't try and deny it," Becky said hotly. "I'm not the only one who thinks so, either. And furthermore, you seem to have totally forgotten about The Party Line. Not only did you blow us off about Sharon's party, you didn't even bother to show up at our regular meeting yesterday afternoon!"

All of a sudden I wanted to melt into the pavement. I'd been so busy practicing with Ms. Thomason that the weekly Party Line meeting had entirely slipped my mind!

I couldn't think of anything to say. I felt so ashamed of myself.

"I thought the four of us were supposed to be partners," Becky said, sounding half angry and half sad.

"We *are* partners!" I managed.

"That's not how it feels anymore. It feels like three partners and one person who thinks she's too good for us because she's in a singing contest."

"Oh, no, Becky, I don't think that!"

"Well, that's how it seems to us," Becky said.

It felt so terrible to have my friends think I was stuck-up, to have them think The Party Line wasn't important to me! I gulped and tried to speak. "I . . . I'm sorry. I d-didn't mean to s-stop d-doing my share. . . ."

I stopped talking, completely mortified. I was so upset I was stuttering. As if that weren't bad enough, I could feel tears coming to my eyes. I did my best to brush them away without Becky seeing.

We walked along in silence, and I kept my head turned away from her. Everything looked blurry through my tears. What good was it to do well in the talent competition or to maybe have my first boyfriend if my three best friends hated me?

I was trying desperately not to cry, but Becky's known me for a long time. After we had walked another block Becky reached into her purse and handed me a tissue, still without looking at me. I took it silently and blew my nose. Finally she turned to me and sighed. "Oh, Allie, I can't stay mad at you. I'm sorry I talked to you that way. I know you had to spend time practicing. It's just that usually we do everything together, and—well, since you've been so busy, I've felt kind of left out."

"It's my fault. I—"

"It's not your fault. I know how important the contest is to you. I just miss you, that's all."

I threw my arms around her, right there on the street. "I couldn't stand that you were mad at me!" I cried.

"I couldn't stand it, either," she said, smiling sheepishly. "Let's just forget it. Deal?"

I grinned from ear to ear. "Deal," I pronounced.

We started talking about school, and about the biology quiz that Ms. Pernell had told us to expect the next day.

"You know, that mnemonic stuff really helped me," said Becky. "I used it in history class to remember the names of the generals in the Civil War. Let's see, bones in the human leg—what was that funny one we thought up before?"

"Hey, I've got another one. Francie Parris Fools Teachers!" I laughed. Francie Parris is a girl in our class. All the teachers love her because she writes such great reports, but all the kids know that she gets her older brother, Ben, to write them for her in exchange for doing all the babysitting he is supposed to do.

"Hey, I told Dylan about our mnemonic technique and he came up with a really great one. Want to hear it?" I asked.

Becky stopped walking and turned to me. "You're doing it again!" she shouted.

I was completely bewildered. "What?"

"Dylan this and Dylan that. I'm sick of it!"

"But Becky—"

"Forget it, Allie. Just forget it."

Becky turned around and stomped off toward the Moondance, leaving me standing by myself on the street. I called out to her once, but she pretended she didn't hear me. And she never looked back.

Nine

I kept wanting to pick up the phone and call Becky, but I didn't have the nerve. Every time the phone rang I thought it would be her, but it never was. Julie and Rosie didn't call me, either. Sure, I saw them at school and they didn't exactly snub me, but it wasn't like before. I didn't know if it would ever be the same with us again. I wanted to do something that would make everything like it used to be, but I had no idea what to do or what to say. My worst fear was that they'd actually kick me out of The Party Line. That would be the most awful thing that could possibly happen to me.

In biology on Thursday I finally gathered up all my courage and walked up to Becky before the bell. I asked her about the quiz we'd taken on the bones in the human leg.

"So how did you do?" I asked her.

"I did okay," she said, not quite meeting my eyes.

"I did okay, too," I said, and that was that. It was a stupid conversation. We both stood there a second, then we both started talking at once.

"Listen—" I said.

"Oh, Allie—" she said at the same time, but just then the bell rang and we had to take our seats. I felt like it had been our opportunity to make up and like we'd both been ready, too, but the moment had passed and it was too late.

I rehearsed a lot with Ms. Thomason, but some of the fun had gone out of it. I still really wanted to do well, but without Becky and Rosie and Julie nothing seemed quite as wonderful.

They didn't even call to wish me luck on the day of the finals. I remembered how Becky had even gotten up extra early to wish me luck the first time. I tried to put it out of my mind and concentrate on the contest. My mom had bought me a beautiful new outfit as a surprise: a pink suede miniskirt and a matching jacket. The outfit was perfect. *Even Rosie would think so . . . if she ever sees it,* I thought sadly.

My whole family went with me to the Canfield Civic Center for the finals. While my family was finding seats, I peeked into the auditorium. My stomach turned over. It seemed like everyone in the entire town was there. I saw Laurie and her boyfriend, Jeff, sitting in the center row. She had on another gorgeous outfit, this time in royal blue velvet. I knew she hadn't made the finals, because Ms. Thomason had read me the list of the finalists. Laurie's name wasn't on it, but Rex's was. I have to admit, that made me feel good. She had been so sure she was better than I was, she had been so sure that Rex was a big nothing, but there we were, getting ready to go on in the finals, and there she was, sitting in the audience. Laurie sat there with her arms folded across her body. She had a nasty scowl on her face. I made a mental note not to look in her direction when I was singing.

I hurried backstage to the warmup room to meet Ms. Thomason.

"Hurry, Allie, we're running late." Ms. Thomason settled herself behind the piano and played a scale for me. "Okay, now. Very lightly, let's hear an arpeggio on la." I sang the notes the way she had taught me, with support from my diaphragm. "Good, Allie. Let's do a couple of scales now." I concentrated on remembering everything she had taught me, and tried not to think about the fact that I, Allison Gray, was about to sing in front of hundreds of people at the Canfield Civic Center! And most of all, I tried to ignore the sad part of me that knew my friends didn't care enough to come hear me sing.

"Good, Allie. You're in fine voice." Ms. Thomason smiled at me. "Well, this is it. I want to tell you that whatever happens, I know you've worked very hard and I respect you for it. Talent isn't enough, Allie. It's what you do with the talent. Remember that."

"I will," I promised.

"Okay, knock 'em dead, Allie!" She gave me a hug and I went to wait with the other four finalists.

Only one other singer was a finalist, and it was Marci. She was standing backstage looking really pretty in a short green corduroy skirt, a pale yellow silk shirt, and a multicolored floral vest. Her curly hair was tied back with a narrow green ribbon.

"Allie! Hi!" she said when she saw me.

"Hi," I said. "You look really great."

"Oh, thanks. My grandparents bought this for me, for luck. I've just been so worried that it's too drab for a performance. I should have worn something like your outfit."

"You look terrific. The pale yellow looks great with your hair," I reassured her.

"I'm so nervous, my hands are numb," she said, reaching for my hand. "Yours is freezing!" she exclaimed when she touched me.

"My hands get cold when I'm scared, too," I said, attempting a smile.

"You know what I do?" said Marci. "I say to myself, 'Okay, Marci, what's the worst thing that could happen to you? You could trip on stage. You could forget your lyrics—' "

"Why do you think like that?" I asked her, horrified.

She held up her hand. "Then I say to myself," she continued, " 'okay, if that happened, would the sun still come up tomorrow? Would your family still be your family and your friends still be your friends? Yes!' So whatever happens can't possibly be that bad!" she concluded triumphantly.

"Does it help?" I asked her.

"No!" she said, laughing. I laughed, too—from nerves, I guess. I didn't want to think too much about the "your friends will still be your friends" part. I didn't know if I still had any friends.

Ms. Rappitz came backstage just as the house lights dimmed. Nervous as I was, I couldn't help noticing her latest ensemble—orange palazzo pants and an orange turtleneck, with an enormous necklace made up of what looked like animal teeth and acorns strung on a piece of leather. It was frightening. Her nose twitched even more than it had at the semifinals. She wore about a zillion jangly bracelets on her extremely thin arms, and she nervously waved her hands in the air as she spoke to the five of us. "I just want to wish you all the best of luck. Remember, whatever happens up there, you are an artist and an artist conducts himself or herself with dignity and aplomb."

"What's aplomb?" piped up a short girl holding a flute. I'd seen her at the semifinals and she was pretty good.

"It means even if you mess up, hold your head up high, and don't ruin my show."

The flautist looked like she wanted to cry, and Ms. Rappitz looked devastated that her attempt at humor had fallen flat. "I was kidding," she assured the flautist, "you'll all be wonderful, I'm sure. So, good luck!" She strode toward the stage, her bracelets jangling with each step.

Marci and I looked at each other, terror written across both of our faces. "Oh, great," she whispered to me. "I feel so much better now."

We could hear Ms. Rappitz on stage, welcoming the crowd. Fortunately they responded a little better to her than we had. They even laughed at one of her jokes.

Marci and I clutched each other's freezing and numb hands as the flautist played her piece. Marci was second, and I wished her luck before she made her entrance. As far as I could tell she sounded great, but I was so terrified it was hard to concentrate on anything.

Third was Elizabeth, the girl who did ballet to the "Moonlight Sonata." I hummed along to the music under my breath, clutching my hands together in my lap. There was a lot of applause for her when she finished, and I could hear her friends whistling and yelling, "Way to go!"

Then it was my turn. Ms. Rappitz introduced me as I stood in the wings, feeling as if my heart were going to burst right out of my chest. As much as I loved to sing, all I could think at that moment was, *Why am I putting myself through this?* It felt like torture!

When Ms. Rappitz said my name, I walked out onto the stage, feeling as if I were on automatic. I think people applauded, but I felt like some kind of robot and the applause didn't really register. I stared out into the audience, my face frozen, as the bright lights hit me. For a moment I was completely blinded. The lights hadn't been like that during the first two stages of the competition. They felt as bright as they had been at the Vermilion concert. I looked into the wings and saw Ms. Rappitz standing in the shadows, her nose twitching away. For one crazy moment she looked just like a giant orange bunny rabbit. Looking at

Ms. Rappitz made me even more terror-stricken, so I whirled my head around, searching for Ms. Thomason's friendly face. She smiled and nodded at me, and even winked. That made me feel a little better, but I was still so nervous I forgot to nod at her to tell her to begin the music. Fortunately, she just started playing. I tried to breathe from my diaphragm, but I couldn't seem to get enough air. Then I heard a little voice from one of the front rows, where I knew my family was sitting. "That's my sister!" the voice said proudly. It was Mouse, bragging about me! I heard my dad go "Shh," but just hearing his voice made me feel better. That was it! I would sing to Mouse again. It had worked before. So what if my friends didn't care about me—I wouldn't let my little brother down.

I took a deep breath and started the first verse.

Somewhere over the rainbow, way up high
There's a land that I've heard of once in a
lullabye.

My voice sounded a little shaky, but I was amazed any sound came out at all. My eyes started getting used to the lights and I could see my family in the audience, their faces beaming. My mom was so nervous, she was mouthing all the words to the song along with me without realizing it.

Whew, I thought when I had made it through the first verse. But as Ms. Thomason played on, I began to pick out other faces in the crowd. I didn't want to look where I knew Laurie Sweet was sitting, so I glanced at the other side of the auditorium. There I saw a bunch of kids from my school: Jennifer Peterson, Liz Barrow, and Cindy Sawyer. And then I saw Becky, Julie, and Rosie, sitting there watching me. Had they come to watch me make a fool out of myself, I wondered. Were they hoping I'd mess up, since I'd been such a rotten friend? Well, I *had* neglected all The Party Line stuff I was supposed to do; what did I expect?

Just as those thoughts flashed through my mind, I looked in the next row and saw Dylan Matthews sitting right next to Mark Harris. Dylan Matthews! I couldn't sing in front of Dylan!

Suddenly I heard Ms. Thomason playing the music to the second verse, and I got a horrible, panicky feeling. It was like being in one of those terrible nightmares, where a monster is chasing you, or where you show up at school and discover you've forgotten to put your clothes on. I couldn't remember a word, not one word, of the second verse to "Over the Rainbow"! Ms. Thomason kept playing, trying to catch my eye, and I just stood there like an idiot, wishing I could fall through a hole in the stage.

I looked over at Ms. Thomason desperately. She could see exactly what had happened. She skipped half the second verse and started playing the music that leads into the third verse. She played the chords very loud and forcefully, I guess hoping that the music would jog my memory. Somehow it worked! Hearing the notes switched on something in my mind, and I sang.

> *Someday I'll wish upon a star*
> *And wake up where the clouds are far behind me.*

Yes, those were the right words! I was back on track, remembering all the words. I hoped my mistake hadn't been too obvious. I figured that unless someone knew the song extremely well, my mistake would have been hard to pick up. That was thanks to Ms. Thomason, who had skipped a few lines of music without making it sound like something was missing. If she hadn't done that I would probably still be standing on that stage with my mouth hanging open.

As I got near the end of the third verse I thought I still sounded nervous, but at least I was singing. And then came the last line. I knew it was almost over, and I gave it all I could.

If happy little bluebirds fly beyond the rainbow,
Why, oh why can't I?

The next thing I knew, everyone was applauding. One part of my mind thought the applause sounded really loud and genuine, but the other part of my mind worried that everyone could tell I had messed up and was just being nice. I figured Laurie Sweet would probably stand up and make an announcement telling everyone I had forgotten the second verse, just in case someone had missed it. Finally the worried part of me won out over the happy part of me and I ran off the stage as quickly as I could, absolutely certain that everyone knew what I had done wrong. I was sure I had looked like the biggest fool in the world, standing there staring out at the crowd for half a verse. My friends would hate me and Dylan would never, ever like me.

The last person to go on was Rex, the Klutzy Magician, but I felt too horrible to pay much attention. I figured if I was going to have a career as a singer, my act would have to be a joke, just like Rex's. I could be Allie, the Terrible Singer.

A madrigal group from Canfield High sang two songs while the judges voted. Then Ms. Rappitz came back to the microphone. "We want to thank all the young people who participated in the

WCAN-TV Talent Search. They all did a wonderful job. At this time I'd like to have our five finalists up on stage."

Oh, no! I thought. *I can't go back up there, I just can't!* But I had to. It would be even worse to be the only one missing. I walked back out there with the other four finalists without saying a word.

"Let's have a round of applause for our talented finalists," Ms. Rappitz said, and everyone clapped. I didn't dare look in the direction of Laurie, who I figured would have a smug, happy look on her face. I didn't dare look at my family or my ex-friends or Dylan Matthews.

"And now it's time to announce our winners. First I want to say that all five of you are really winners for having worked so hard and come so far." I stared at the toes of my pink suede boots while she opened the judges' envelope.

"Honorable mentions go to Rex Chandler and Allison Gray!"

Rex and I walked over to Ms. Rappitz as the audience applauded. She shook both our hands and gave us gift certificates to the record store in the mall. Rex dropped his gift certificate and then tripped over his shoelaces. I wasn't sure if he did it on purpose or not, but everyone laughed.

Ms. Rappitz went on to announce the winners.

Third place went to the girl who played flute, and second place went to the ballet dancer.

"And our grand prize winner, who will appear on WCAN-TV, is Marci Berman!"

Marci stepped forward and, as miserable as I felt, I was happy for her. Not happy enough to stay around to congratulate her, though. As soon as I could, I got off that stage and ran into the bathroom backstage. It was simple: I had decided I was never, ever going to come out.

Ten

I stood in the bathroom waiting for everyone to leave. I knew my parents would be expecting to see me, but I just didn't let myself think about it. Finally it got really quiet backstage. Then it occurred to me, what if I got locked in? Besides, deep down I knew I'd have to come out and face everyone eventually. I went to the sink and threw cold water on my face. Then I brushed my hair, took a deep breath, and went out to face the music.

The auditorium was empty, except for my parents and Mouse standing in the back. My friends had left. *My ex-friends,* I reminded myself. And as for Dylan—well, I'd just never speak to him again before he had a chance to never speak to me again.

I walked over to my parents. "Hi," I said quietly, and then like a complete idiot, I started to cry.

My mom hugged me. "Oh, honey, don't cry. You were wonderful!"

"I wasn't wonderful. I was horrible," I gulped out.

My dad looked completely bewildered. "You were terrific, honey, really! Are you upset because you didn't win?" He handed me his handkerchief.

"Not because I didn't win. I just wanted to do my best."

"And you did," he assured me.

"No, I didn't," I said, blowing my nose. "I messed up the whole second verse. You're just being nice."

My father really looked bewildered. "Sweetie, I'm not just being nice. I mean it. I don't know what you're talking about."

I wiped at my eyes and looked closely at his face. My dad has one of those faces where you can see everything, and besides, he never lies to me. I could see he was telling the truth. Was it actually possible that the whole world didn't know I had messed up?

"Really?" I asked. "Because I wouldn't blame you if you wanted to disown me."

In spite of their concern for me, my parents smiled at each other. Then my father gave me an enormous hug and my mother stroked my hair.

"Allie, you sang beautifully, and we've never been prouder of you," Mom said. "So you got nervous and forgot a verse—it happens to everyone,

even big stars. Ms. Thomason could tell you that!
It just means you're human."

"Anyways, *I* thought you sang wonderful,"
Mouse said with a very serious look on his face.

I hugged him. He can be a royal pain, sometimes, but he really is a sweet kid.

Dad stepped back and picked up my coat. "Come
on, sweetie," he said gently. "Let's go home."

On the way home Mouse kept chattering about
the new guinea pig at his preschool. The class had
named the guinea pig Morris. Mouse was really
excited because his teacher had said that he would
be able to have a turn to bring the guinea pig
home overnight.

"And you know what, Allie? I almost got him
for tonight! Then Morris would have been—"

"—in the way!" my mother finished quickly.
"We just wanted to concentrate on you tonight,"
she added, smiling at me.

Mouse chattered on but I didn't pay much attention. I couldn't help noticing that Mike, Caroline,
and Suzanne had left before I'd come out of the
bathroom. I started to worry again that everyone
really did know I had forgotten some of the words.
I felt like a total jerk, and I stared into the night
as we headed for home.

When we walked into the darkened house, I was
thinking that all I had to look forward to was

catching up on a ton of homework. Then all of a sudden, the hall light switched on and about a million people jumped out of the living room and yelled, *"Surprise!"* The next thing I knew, everyone was laughing and yelling.

"Turn around! Turn around!" yelled Mouse, jumping up and down. I turned around, and across the stairway was a huge sign that read, We Love You, Allie.

"Isn't the sign great?" Mouse yelped. "I helped do it!"

"Are you surprised, honey?" my mom asked. She ruffled Mouse's hair. "This little guy almost gave the whole thing away in the car!"

"I just wanted Morris to come to the party," Mouse explained.

Before I could say anything to Mouse, the crowd parted and three people came forward—Rosie, Julie, and Becky, with huge grins on their faces. They hugged me, and I started crying all over again. In public, even!

"Stop crying!" Rosie laughed. "Red, blotchy skin doesn't go with pink suede—which, by the way, looks totally wicked."

"How? When?" I stammered.

"It was Becky's idea," Julie explained. "Are you really surprised?"

I laughed. "I've never been so surprised in my life!"

Becky looked at me, her eyes shining. "We're so proud of you, and we just want you to know that."

"But I—"

"But nothing," Becky said firmly. "You were terrific."

Ms. Thomason stepped forward out of the crowd. "Allie, in honor of this special occasion we all got together and got you something to remember it by." She handed me a small white box and a card. I opened the card first. The front said, "The whole gang just wants to let you know," and the inside read, "You're terrific!" It was signed all over the inside and on the back by my whole family and all my friends.

"Open it! Open it!" Mouse cried, jumping up and down. "It's a—"

Caroline clamped her hand over his mouth. "Don't give it away, silly!"

I untied the pink ribbon and opened the white box. Inside it was a blue velvet box. I snapped open the box and gasped. Nestled inside was a thin gold chain with a musical note on it. A tiny diamond glistened in the center of the note. It was so beautiful! My hands shook a little as I took it out of the box.

"Here, I'll help you," my mom said. She lifted my hair and fastened the chain around my neck.

I was overwhelmed. I didn't feel like I deserved such a wonderful present. But it was as if Ms. Thomason could hear what I was thinking. She touched my arm gently, and I looked at her through the tears in my eyes. "Remember what I told you, Allie. To have talent isn't enough. Most people are too scared to try the things they'd like to do. But you did try, and now you know you'll keep on trying, and get better and better. Right?"

"Right!" I said, wiping the tears from my eyes.

"Enough of this mushy stuff!" yelled my brother Mike. "Let's eat!"

Everyone laughed and started talking at once. My parents went to set out the food.

Then, out of the corner of my eye, I saw him. Dylan Matthews was at my surprise party!

He walked over to me. "Hi," he said shyly.

I tugged at the pink ribbon that was still in my hands. "Hi."

"So, I finally got to hear you sing," he said.

"Yeah. I wasn't very good," I murmured, looking down.

"Are you kidding? I thought you were terrific!" he said.

"You didn't notice?" I asked him.

"Notice what?"

"I forgot some of the words. In the second verse, I mean."

"Oh, that," he said. "I thought it was just a different arrangement of the song."

"Really?" I asked him, amazed.

"Really," he assured me. "Besides, that can happen to anyone. I've seen it happen lots of times to my sister, Megan. Once she was a soloist in this huge summer concert in the park, and just when she opened her mouth to sing, a huge bug flew down her throat."

"Oh, no!" I shrieked. "What did she do?"

"Well, she tried to sing anyway, but it just came out as kind of a gurgle. And then she got so freaked out she forgot the words to her solo completely, so she just stood there and gurgled!"

"Oh, gee, oh, that's horrible," I said, but I couldn't stop laughing at the thought of his sister trying to sing with a bug in her throat.

"Anyway, she went on to get a music scholarship and everything," he finished.

I smiled at him gratefully.

Julie came over with a plate full of food. "Yum, your parents cooked up a storm," she said as she began eating.

Mark walked over with a full plate and sat down next to her. Julie looked down at her plate, her mouth full of food, and I could tell she was worrying about her braces and debating whether or not to eat in front of Mark. Finally her appetite won out over her self-consciousness. She caught my eye and shrugged, then dug in.

"Hey, Allie, you were great," said Mark, as he forked up my mom's special potato salad. "And so's this potato salad." I laughed. Evidently Mark and Julie had something in common besides sports—they both loved to eat!

"Hungry?" Dylan asked me.

I smiled at him. "I'm starved!"

The nicest boy in my class walked me over to the buffet table my parents had set up. *Maybe life isn't so bad after all,* I decided.

Eleven

Dylan and I each had two hamburgers, two help-
ings of my mom's famous potato salad, and two
pieces of chocolate cake. Mark and Julie each had
three pieces of cake! Caroline put on the new Bas-
tille album, "Rocket Rock," and Julie hummed
along as she devoured her third piece of cake. She
and Rosie knew every song on the album by heart.
Some of the older kids started to dance.

Every once in a while I'd watch Becky across
the room. I felt like I still really needed to talk to
her. I saw her talking to my mom, and then she
walked over to Rosie and said something. I saw
Rosie nod. Then Becky came over to where Julie
and I were sitting in the living room.

"I'm stuffed," she said, holding her stomach.
"Your mom really outdid herself."

"You won't get any argument from me," I said,
polishing off the last of my chocolate cake.

Becky looked at Julie, then at me. "Hey, come on outside for a minute, okay?"

Julie said "Sure thing, if I can still move," and got up from her chair. I looked over at Dylan, who was sitting on the couch next to me. "Excuse me," I said.

"Will your mom mind if I sneak thirds?" he asked.

I laughed. "She'll want to adopt you. She loves to feed people."

Becky, Julie, and I went to the side door, where Rosie was waiting for us.

The four of us walked outside and started down the block. The party sounds faded as we got further from the house. It felt great to be with my friends again, but I didn't quite know what to say. There was so much I wanted to tell them.

"Listen, you guys," I finally said, "I never want anything to come between us again."

"I agree!" said Rosie.

"But it will," Becky said with a sigh. I could tell she was searching for the right words. "I mean, sometimes one of us will get involved in stuff that doesn't involve all of us, and it'll be hard."

"And then there's boys," said Julie.

"Yeah, boys," sighed Becky.

"But a boyfriend isn't more important than a girlfriend," I stated vehemently, and Becky smiled at me.

"I agree," said Julie. "I hate it when Heather breaks a date with her girlfriends just because of some guy."

"It's much better to play hard to get," Rosie advised.

"No, that's not the point," said Julie. "It's just a dumb thing to do. It's like saying boys are more important than girls."

"Yeah, I see what you mean," Rosie agreed.

"Let's promise each other right now," I said impetuously, "that we won't ever break dates with each other for a boy."

"Ever?" asked Rosie, looking skeptical.

"Ever," I pronounced.

She smiled. "You're right. Ever."

"And we'll try not to let anything get in the way of The Party Line," Becky added, looking at me. "It's a business, and our clients depend on us. And more important, we don't want to let one another down."

I nodded solemnly and Becky continued, "But if something does interfere with The Party Line, something really, truly important, then we should try to understand. Agreed?"

I smiled at Becky. "Agreed!" we all called out.

Then we all put our hands in the center of a circle, one on top of another. Rosie looked at me. "Is this juvenile or what?" she asked me.

"No," I said firmly. "This is important." Then with our hands on top of one another's we repeated the two promises we had just made. I felt like a huge load had been lifted off my shoulders.

"Hey, race you back to the house!" Rosie yelled.

As usual, Julie took off after Rosie. I looked at Becky and laughed. "She always does that because she knows she'll win," I said ruefully.

Becky laughed, too. "And she always does."

We started walking back to the house. In the distance I could hear the happy voices and the music from my party. It felt so good to be with Becky again.

"I'm glad the contest is over," I said.

"You were terrific. I haven't had a chance to tell you."

"Not so terrific. I guess you know how I messed up."

Becky nodded. "Yeah, I knew, but that's only because 'Over the Rainbow' is my mother's all-time favorite song, and she sings it all the time. If I hadn't known the song so well I never would have been able to tell."

I stopped and turned to her. I knew Becky wouldn't lie to me. "Really? You don't think everyone knew?"

"I'm sure they didn't. I heard lots of people saying how great your voice was, people who don't even know you."

Imagine that: people who don't even know me know my voice. What a wonderful thought.

When we got back to my house, Ms. Thomason was sitting in the center of a group of people. They had just been singing songs.

"Sing more!" Mouse yelled. He went over to Ms. Thomason and plopped himself on her lap. But Ms. Thomason must have seen me come in, because she started singing "Over the Rainbow." Everyone looked around for me, until all eyes were on me. Dylan was standing right near the couch, and he smiled at me. I looked around at my family and at my three best friends. Then I marched over to where Ms. Thomason and Mouse were sitting, and I sang "Over the Rainbow" from beginning to end. I didn't forget any of the lyrics and I sang every note right, even the hard ones at the end.

If happy little bluebirds fly beyond the rainbow,
Why, oh why can't I?

And right then, with all my family and friends standing there in my living room, with that beautiful gold necklace around my neck, I knew I couldn't be any happier even if I really could fly over the rainbow. I knew one day I would be a singer. And I wasn't afraid at all.

SPECIAL PARTY TIP
Allie's Theme Cookies

Special cookies make a great finishing touch for a theme party. Of course it's very convenient if you can find cookie cutters in the right shape, like we did for Patti's roller-skating party. But even if you can't find the perfect shape, don't worry. You can always make a cardboard pattern and just trace around it with a sharp knife. All you need to do is think of a shape to match your theme: hearts for Valentine's Day, pumpkins for Halloween—you get the idea. Then follow any recipe for sugar cookie dough, roll it out with a rolling pin, and start cutting out the shapes. Once you've baked the cookies, you can start in on the really fun part, decorating. For our roller-skate cookies, we used white icing for the boot and chocolate for the wheels. They looked great, but they tasted even better!

Of course, it isn't always easy to figure out a good shape that fits a party theme. It might be a little too complicated, for instance, to bake a cookie shaped like a clown for a circus party. So decorate a plain cookie to match your theme! Just use a glass to cut out dough circles and, once they're baked, use icing to make a big round clown face on each. On a round shape, you can use icing to "paint" a baseball, a record album, a dartboard or even a pizza! You can use other shapes, too, like squares and triangles. The only limit is your imagination.

One day Allie, Rosie, Becky and Julie saved a birthday party from becoming a complete disaster. The next day, the four best friends are running their own business...

Don't miss these Party Line Adventures!

by Carrie Austen

___#1: ALLIE'S WILD SURPRISE 0-425-12047-3/$2.75

Allie's favorite rock star is in town, but how will she get the money for a concert ticket? When the clown hired for her little brother's birthday party is a no-show, Allie finds her miracle! Before you can say "make a wish," the girls are in the party business--having fun and getting paid for it! Can The Party Line make Allie's rock concert a dream come true?

___#2: JULIE'S BOY PROBLEM 0-425-12048-1/$2.75

It's hard to get a romance going with the cute Mark Harris when his best friend, Casey Wyatt, is an obnoxious girl-hater. Then, in the misunderstanding of the century, The Party Line gets hired to give a party for Casey. When Casey finds out, it's all-out war.

___#3: BECKY'S SUPER SECRET 0-425-12131-3/$2.75

Becky is putting together a top secret mystery party and she'll need her three best friends to help her do it in style. The only problem is: Becky hasn't exactly told them yet that they're going to help. Can Becky pull off the surprise party of the year?

___#4: ROSIE'S POPULARITY PLAN 0-425-12169-0/$2.75

It's just Rosie's luck to get paired with Jennifer--the weird new girl--for an English project. Next, Jennifer's mom thinks it would be a great idea if The Party Line threw a birthday party for Jennifer. The rest of the girls will need some serious convincing!

It's where everything happens!
by Ann Hodgman

___#1: NIGHT OF A THOUSAND PIZZAS 0-425-12091-0/$2.75

It all started with the school lunchroom's brand new, computerized pizza maker. Instead of one-hundred pizzas, the cook accidentally programmed it to make one thousand! What can the kids do? Have you ever tried to get rid of a thousand extra-large pizzas?

___#2: FROG PUNCH 0-425-12092-9/$2.75

This time the principal has gone too far. Ballroom dancing lessons. UGH! Even worse, he's planned a formal dance. Now the sixth grade is determined to fight back. When they unleash their secret weapon in the lunchroom, things will go completely bonkers!

___#3: THE COOKIE CAPER 0-425-12132-1/$2.75

The kids want to sell their baked cookies to raise money for the class treasury. But where will they find a kitchen big enough? The lunchroom! The cookies turn out to be so amazing the kids at Hollis get to be on TV, but the baking business turns out to be more than *anybody* needed!

___#4: THE FRENCH FRY ALIENS
0-425-12170-4/$2.75

It's going to be super scary when the kids give their performance of the class play. Especially since the sixth grade's all-new *Peter Pan* looks like it may turn into The French Fry Aliens—an interplanetary mess!